HOLIDAY GAMES

A Sexy Snowed-in Holiday Novella

CAT WYNN

Jingle bells all the way home

Cat Wynn

Holiday Games

Cover Design By: Cover Apothecary at coverapothecary.com

Editor: Brittni Van at Overbooked Author Services

To me and to Griff, a very good judge of character

Chapter 1

AFTER THE WORST YEAR OF HER LIFE, AUGUST POINTE WAS determined to have the best Christmas of her life. She rubbed her hands together as she surveyed the neatly stocked shelves of her Uncle Joe's built-in designer refrigerator that seamlessly disappeared amongst the kitchen's custom walnut panels.

Uncle Joe had offered his Asheville mountain house for August and her friends to spend a Friendsmas together after August spilled her guts about a...*work incident* that had been plaguing her for months.

The work situation had finally come to a head thus creating the worst year of August's life and the need for a fun holiday ASAP. She'd always been Uncle Joe's favorite niece, and so the use of the fancy house was a gift to cheer her up.

House was an understatement, though. Really it was closer to a mansion, making her own apartment twenty miles away seem laughably small.

The downstairs was open but cozy with overstuffed leather couches, high vaulted ceilings with exposed wood beams, and a large stone encased fireplace. The upstairs had seven bedrooms, all with attached bathrooms. And the kitchen had floor to ceiling windows overlooking the white and verdant rolling peaks of the Appalachians. Holly was twisted around the banisters, and gold and silver decorated the red spruces located in many of the rooms.

Plus, the exterior of the house had been professionally decorated for the holidays, with white icicle lights hanging from the slanted shingles on the roof and oversized glittery metallic ornaments dipping the branches of the cluster of Yellow Birch and White Ash in the front.

August was breathless at the sight when she rolled up the evening before, especially as soft flakes fell from the sky, dusting every surface of nature with a thick veneer of a wintry iridescent white. She came early so she could make sure every-thing was perfect before her friends arrived. She liked to be prepared.

As she was turning out the labels of every bottled item in the fridge, she paused at the sound of the Christmas Carol doorbell.

We wish you a merry Christmas
We wish you a merry Christmas
We wish you a merry Christmas…

She checked her phone: one thirty five pm. Seemingly too early for her friends Olivia and Elliot to arrive, who never showed up early to a damn thing. But maybe Christmas mira-cles really did happen? She rushed out of the kitchen and through the living room to the front of the house.

And a happy new year!

She smoothed out her fitted red sweater and swung open the door.

"Merry Christ—oh fuck." Her words caught in her throat.

Instead of her friends, a tall man in a dark green knit cap and a messy mop of hair stood in front of her. Where was that taser her dad had gifted her when she'd moved into her apart-ment? Dammit, it was in a locked box under her bed twenty miles away.

The man gave her a disarming smile which turned into an

expectant look. He cleared his throat. "Jack. Jack Harris. Olivia's friend."

"Jack? Oh! Jack!" When she said the words they finally registered in her brain. Olivia had invited her old friend Jack at the last minute to spend the holidays with them. Olivia and Jack used to bartend together in Charleston, where Olivia lived. It was very weird for Olivia to invite Jack into their personal Friendsmas in August's opinion, but Olivia loved to pick up strays, and she was the kind of person who was always making new friends and nonchalantly inviting them into the inner circle. Bringing people together was one of Olivia's special talents, alienating strangers was one of August's.

August's eyes traveled to a small grey pom pom of fluff peeping out of the crook of Jack's arm, and she almost jumped. "Oh my god, what's that?"

"You've never seen a kitten before?" He asked with genuine surprise. He also spoke with a vague Southern lilt which was pleasant to the ear. The kitten's two peaked ears stuck out like crests of a mountain top. Its smoky fur was frosted with melting snow from the storm outside.

"I know what a fucking cat is…" August mumbled, but waved Jack in. "Jesus, get inside. Olivia won't arrive for another two hours. Also, we're not supposed to have pets here." Not a strict rule, per say, but her uncle was a stickler, and August had never had a pet in her entire life aside from that betta fish she rehomed to Elliot in college.

"This little guy?" He gestured to the kitten in his arms and stomped his shoes against the mat outside the door then stepped through the threshold, toeing off his boots before lining them up on the mat next to the entryway. "I found her under the porch, so technically she already lived here."

When he unzipped his coat, he gently traded the kitten from one arm to another, then shrugged out of the sleeves, revealing broad shoulders encased in a grey hoodie. She averted her gaze when interest in the hard plane of his chest sparked a little too hot in her sternum.

Don't start with your weird awkwardness now! She fiddled with the hem of her shirt, shaking the visual of his body out of her brain, tossing her wavy brown hair from her shoulders. "You're really early. I thought you were coming with Olivia."

"Yeah…" His voice trailed. His footsteps were light as he followed behind her to the couch. "Olivia was supposed to pick me up along the way, but she texted she was running late with a client. So, I checked the weather map, and it's supposed to get pretty gnarly out there. I planned accordingly and left early. It's not a bad drive for me, but the snow fall's only gonna get worse throughout the night. Olivia said she'd let you know."

"Information sharing isn't one of Olivia's specialties. Would've been nice to know about the kitten in advance too…"

"To be fair, I didn't know about the kitten in advance."

"Yes. I suppose that is fair." She cleared her throat. "Well, I don't know what she's going to eat. The refrigerator is stocked but not with anything appropriate for a fucking *kitten.* Maybe the smoked oysters or tinned fish. But that's expensive."

He looked a little sheepish. "I have some stuff out in my truck. I also brought some groceries, hope you don't mind. I like pulling my weight in the kitchen. I'm a chef."

She raised her eyebrow. "A chef with cat food in his car?"

He pulled off his knit cap and scratched at his messy mop of dark brown hair, almost as if embarrassed. Light caught the color, dashing it with deep auburn red. "I volunteer at an animal shelter. Foster some kittens, that kind of thing. They're real sweet, you know?" He lifted the kitten up towards his face and planted a kiss on her little head. "She picked the right guy. I'd say she's about ten weeks, maybe just weaned from her mom."

Heat lifted to August's cheeks, something felt strangely intimate about the tiny kiss he'd planted on the kitten's head. "Oh."

"Wanna hold her?" He leaned forward a bit as if that would tempt her with proximity. But she leaned back, like a magnet repelling another magnet. The small kitten turned its little unblinking gaze on her. Such a tiny creature so gently engulfed in such large, strong arms...

Don't be weird!

She scoffed. "No. Besides, it probably has fleas and worms and all kinds of disgusting things." She patted her jean pocket, and slid out her phone. "The bedrooms are up the stairs. We'll have to figure something out for that animal later—"

"No worries, I have something figured out."

What could he possibly have figured out? August pursed her lips. "Fine. Well, since you're here early, you get your pick of the rooms. I'll be right back." She had to call Olivia immediately. *And murder her for leaving her all alone with this handsome, dumb man and small, useless probably filthy kitten!*

Maybe for Olivia or Elliot, hanging out with this, albeit handsome man, would be good, old fashioned holiday fun. But August didn't have the charisma, the natural flirtation. Awkward one-on-one interactions made her skin physically itch. She wasn't good at feigning interest. Or smiling when she didn't mean it. Everyone at work referred to her as an ice queen, and that wasn't wrong. But that icy exterior was protection against the constant pain of scalding, uncomfortable, needling human interaction.

Sorry, Brenda from marketing. *I'd rather spend Christmas in the eye of a volcano than hear you blather on about what you did over the weekend with your shitty husband who hasn't washed a dish in five years.*

She stomped off to her room, which happened to be the master suite. August wouldn't have taken it since she lived the nearest to the house and therefore had the shortest distance to travel, but her friends insisted even though Olivia was in Charleston and Elliot was in…

Actually, she wasn't so sure where Elliot was staying at the moment. Chicago maybe? As a traveling photographer, Elliot was in a new city every week.

Still, It wasn't always easy being friends with August, she was aware. But Olivia and Elliot had accepted her, regardless. Never questioned her crankiness, or her shortness, her social ineptitude. In fact, they seemed to even appreciate it. So, best Christmas ever? Yes, she had to deliver. *For friendship.*

She tapped her fingernails against the dresser next to the large window overlooking the scenic Blue Ridge backdrop. Snow fell in aggressive flakes, cutting diagonally across the balcony. She smashed her phone against her ear as it rang several times until Olivia picked up. Before August could say a word Olivia was talking a mile a minute, her voice frantic instead of its usual cheery lilt.

"Holy fucking shit, August you won't fucking believe what it looks like out here. We're pretty much stranded."

"We're not stranded yet, we're in the Celebration Inn parking lot." A deep and familiar voice sounded from the other end of the call.

August switched the phone to the other ear, pressing her forehead against the cool glass of the window to quell her bubbling panic. "Who's that? Is that Henry?"

Henry was August's older brother. And he wasn't supposed to be coming on this trip. While August and Henry possessed similar personality traits, those traits were executed very differently. For example, Henry was a cardiothoracic surgical resident, one who was often too busy to spend holidays with friends and family. And August was afraid of the sight of blood.

"I thought you were driving yourself after your last client." Olivia was a hair stylist. One so popular and in demand, that her clientele were celebrities and other wealthy people. They often required extra special treatment, of course.

"Girl, I was, but that bastard kept me forty five minutes late, and so I didn't have time to run home to get any of my things. Henry picked them up for me so I hitched a ride with him. Easy peasy."

"So, Henry's spending Christmas with us?" Henry and Olivia lived in the same building in Charleston and they had a weird love-hate relationship going on that August wanted to know absolutely nothing about.

"Duh. He's your brother. Wait, Henry wasn't invited?" *Um, no.* But then Olivia was frantic again. "Oh! Oh! The cops just rolled up. Shit. *Shit.*"

August squeezed her eyes shut. "Don't tell me."

"They're shutting down the roads."

"You're kidding."

"At least we're already at a hotel. See! Safety first!"

"Olivia…" August said through gritted teeth. "I'm here *alone* with your friend Jack who is a complete and total stranger to me. You can't leave me with this himbo!"

"Oh, Jack made it already, that's so exciting! Himbo, yes. That's a good word for him."

"Who's Jack?" Henry's voice came from a distance.

Then Olivia's voice reduced to a whisper. "Isn't he so unbelievably hot? Super nice too, I'm so happy he made it."

"Who *is* Jack?" Henry's voice sounded again in the background.

"Well, I'm *not* so happy he made it," August hissed. "You know I'm not good with small talk. Or strangers! Fuck. *Fuck.* This trip was supposed to be about us. You, me, and Elliot. It was supposed to be absolutely perfect. And now Henry. And this snowstorm. And…*Jack.* Elliot better get here, stat."

But Olivia didn't respond, instead her voice muffled as if she'd covered the phone with her palm, but August could still hear her. "Should we be worried? Parking lot's chaos...I forgot to pack my mittens."

"What'd you say?"

Olivia's voice returned to normal. "It's not looking good, August. I don't think we're gonna make it tonight."

"You can't leave me here with that man." The creep of desperation tinged her voice. "He brought a wild animal into the house."

"Exsqueeze me? Like what? A rat? A racoon?"

She leaned over, cupping the phone. "No...he brought a...he brought a *kitten*," she whispered.

August pursed her lips when she heard chuckling on the line. "Oh no, the handsome TikTok famous chef brought a kitten to the holiday mountain house."

August sighed. "Can you try to have a little sympathy? I'm not like you. This is really uncomfortable for me."

At that Olivia's tone changed. "Sweetie, sweetie, sweetie. I know it's not ideal, and I want to be there just as much as you. Do you think I'm happy about missing our first get together in three years? I'm just trying to keep up a good attitude. And look, I'm not god, I can't account for mother nature. If we try to drive ninety miles in this weather, we're probably gonna die. So take your pick. Do you want that blood on your hands? Or would you rather hang out with a handsome dude and a kitten for a while? Might I remind you, your guilt is even stronger than your awkwardness. Just have him feed you, he's an amazing chef."

August rolled from her forehead to the back of her head, her gaze now on the stark white ceiling. When she spoke, she was surprised at how childlike her voice sounded. "You're right. I just want everyone to be safe. I'll text Elliot. Elliot can make her way through anything. Right?"

"I'm sure you're right." But Olivia didn't sound sure. "Gotta call you back. Everyone's making a mad rush for the

Celebration Inn now. Shit! Henry, get out and run in front of that crowd! Can you get me a room with a view of the pool?"

"Okay, text me in the morning!" August shouted into the phone but Olivia was already gone. She hung up and shoved her phone back into her pocket.

It was going to be okay, *deep breath*. There was always a chance Elliot would turn up despite the odds. *Especially Elliot.* She was already traveling all the time anyway, and she was crafty as hell.

They'd all met in college, but Elliot had dropped out before the end of sophomore year. Not that it mattered, she was successful and glamorous all the same. Most of which had to do with her devil-may-care attitude. Surely, a snowstorm was no match for Elliot Sheer.

In the distance, August's ears perked at the sound of the front door opening and closing.

She could be friendly with a stranger. She'd have to be a big girl and suck it up. She straightened her shoulders and walked out to the hallway and down the stairs to the living room. But then she froze at the sight of Jack in the corner of the room. "What's all this?" she asked.

Chapter 2

JACK WAS KNEELING, BENT OVER A SMALL NET COVERED enclosure, similar to a miniature tent. He raised his head at her voice and gave another disarming smile. This guy smiled *a lot*. She'd never known a man to smile so much. "I made a spot for Holiday. Should keep her safe until I can take her home and bring her to the vet." He fluffed around some fleece blankets with blue and white printed snowflakes and red and green plaid.

"Holiday?"

"Yeah, that's what I've named her. I didn't wanna name her Christmas because I don't know what she celebrates."

August put her hands on her forehead. *Goddammit.* That really was pretty sweet. And she'd been bitching about the kitten before. She sidled closer. "Is she...okay?" It's not like she wanted harm to come to a helpless kitten. But she also didn't want to take care of it... She had enough to deal with in her own life.

Jack arranged two small bowls in the pen, one with water and the other with mushy looking meat. "Oh yeah, she'll be just fine. A little exhausted, some rest and food is in order. She has a lot of fight in her. When she was under the deck, she screamed as soon as I placed my foot on the first step.. Like she knew I'd save her."

August huffed. "But she didn't make any noise when I arrived."

Jack nestled another thick fleece blanket into the pen, where August even spotted a make-shift litter box fashioned out of a shoebox. He shrugged. "Maybe she didn't hear you. Or maybe she just knows I'm a sucker. Animals can sense things like that."

August's eyebrows knitted together. "Why wouldn't she think that *I* would pick her up?" She was a good person. Wait —*was she?* She had wondered this about herself a lot lately. Still...this kitten knew something about August. She knew August wouldn't be capable of taking care of her properly. The thought made her spine stiffen a little. "You know what, don't answer that question."

Reflexively, she reached for her phone, tapping out a message.

August: HELP ME

Typing bubbles appeared almost instantly.

Elliot Sheer: You will not believe how hot this guy is standing in front of me at the airport. How's it going over there? You good?

Yes! Elliot was going to pull through for August. August picked up her phone to call. "I'll be back," she said to Jack, and stalked back to her bedroom, plopping down on the edge of her King sized bed.

Instead of answering, Elliot switched to video chat, her alabaster skin and shining black hair bright on August's phone screen. "Shut up, shut up, shut up!" Elliot whispered-hissed.

August looked left and right. "I'm not saying anything!"

Then Elliot flipped her screen so it was facing the back of the man several feet in front of her in line at her terminal's gate. "August, this is the hottest man I've ever seen."

August squinted her eyes. The man in front of Elliot was clearly tall with broad shoulders, a head of thick ashy brown hair that was cut neat and short at his neck. Other than that, he could've been anyone. He wore a simple grey shirt and jeans. The screen flipped back to Elliot. "Think he wants to join the Mile High Club?"

August gave an incredulous look. "He just looks like..a man. All you showed me was the back of his head. And can't he hear you?"

Elliot shook her head. "Nah, too much noise here. I caught a glimpse of his ticket. First name's Parker. Not sure how I feel about that name. Is that a hot name? All depends on his last name I suppose."

"I'd say sixty-six percent on the hot scale. The important thing is, you're on your way to Asheville, right? The weather's not great, so I'm worried. Olivia and Henry are stranded, but they're coming from the opposite direction."

"Sure, I've flown through worse than this…" But then Elliot's voice trailed off, her bright blue gaze distracted, her head turned a touch and August could hear the muffled sounds of an overhead speaker. "Ahhhh…speak of the devil and she shall appear. Strike that, Augie. Flight's canceled. Mother*fucker*."

August squeezed her eyes shut. "Elliot."

"August."

"I'm stuck here all by myself!"

"But you love being by yourself!"

August fell back on the bed. "That wasn't the point of this trip. And this guy Jack is here too, and you know I'm awkward."

"Wait, Jack…Olivia's friend? I totally forgot he was coming."

"Yeah, he was on that one group email."

Elliot nodded. "Right, right. I follow him on Tiktok. He's that hot chef that specializes in that overpriced elevated comfort food. He didn't follow me back though, which is super weird. Most men wanna slide in your DMs right away, you know?"

"Elliot, pay attention. What am I gonna do?"

Elliot gave a cheeky smile but still her tone had softened. "Get drunk, obvi. Then live your best life. It's Christmas. A little social lubrication never hurt nobody. Tipsy August is like the most fun you ever become. Sorry. Gotta go, I gotta get my flights in order. Maybe I can get out tonight? Tomorrow? No promises, okay byeeee!"

"Wait, no don't go!" August sat up, almost shouting into the phone.

But the screen went black.

Her friends had abandoned her with *Jack*. Oh, and Holiday. The *fucking kitten* who may or may not celebrate Christmas. Everything was supposed to be perfect! This was the Christmas that would make up for the horrible thing that had happened…August shook her head. *Nope!* She wouldn't think about that now.

This time when she marched into the living room no one was there. Not Jack and not the kitten.

She leaned over the small pen to see it emptied. "Hello?" she called.

Then a voice came from the other side of the hallway. "Hey! In the kitchen."

She peered over the corner wall that separated the two rooms to see Jack rummaging through the refrigerator, as he put away the items he'd brought in from his big reusable bag of groceries. The bag itself was insulated and heavy duty. She watched with interest as he unpacked paper wrapped packages of sausage, wheels of French cheese, small glass jars of artisanal goods.

"My uncle filled the fridge so I can't imagine there's anything else you might need."

He glanced over his shoulder, his words easy. "Yeah, but I'd rather be puréed in a blender than go anywhere without my hot chili honey. Make it myself. But I did already scope out the liquor collection, not too shabby. So, I'd say…" He grabbed a large mixing glass from the freezer and gave it a fancy toss, catching it after he flipped in the air. "It's the perfect time for a drink. You know, if you're into it."

Chapter 3

AUGUST THOUGHT ABOUT ELLIOT'S WORDS: *GET DRUNK, OBVI.* Was there ever better advice in the history of advice? At the very least, a drink or two did loosen August up a bit.

Cautiously, she sidled up to the kitchen counter, resting her elbows on the smooth surface, keeping her eyes on Jack. She had to admit that he was…incredibly hot, which *leave it to Olivia to bring a random hot man into the group and not think twice about it.*

He was certainly hotter than any of the men she hung around. Mostly men from work. All of them accountants like her. And not a hot one in the bunch.

In that moment, she desperately wished she was sexy and carefree like Olivia or bold and funny like Elliot. But she was August: stiff and bitchy. But she'd mixed a drink or two in college. She could be normal.

"I can make drinks," she said. "You're my guest, after all. I want you to feel welcomed."

He lifted his brows and handed her the glass. "Well, then."

August waved it away. Honestly, she didn't know what to do with it anyway. At home, she mostly drank wine, rose, or vodka tonics. Easy and didn't require her to be a cool mixologist.

But she did recall a drink Elliot used to make them all in college. It was a strong one, which she figured had to be suitable for the occasion. And it had lots of ingredients which would indicate she knew what she was doing.

She'd only spent brief moments with Jack but the hipness emanated from him like the spicy warm waft of a freshly baked gingerbread. Even now, his long form was leaned against the countertop, hand on a trim hip, head tipped affably, hair mussed just so. But his face had just the hint of a challenging smirk on it.

Hmm. August turned to the tall pantry where her uncle had generously provided them with all manners of expensive liquor. "Let me gather my ingredients."

She began pulling from the shelves, cradling the bottles in her arms: gin, tequila, vodka, triple sec, rum. Then placed them one by one on the counter, displaying each bottle with the labels facing out. She acquired two tall glasses from the glass windowed cabinet behind her, filled them with crushed ice from the special freezer under the counter, and placed them on the countertop as well.

Now it's time for some mixology.

If she recalled correctly, Elliot used to eyeball the distribution of liquor but August knew the gist.

Half an ounce of the gin.

Half an ounce of tequila.

Half an ounce of vodka—*oops, a little heavy on that pour.*

Half an ounce of triple sec.

Half an ounce of rum.

And the glass was nearly filled to the brim. Still, she was forgetting something. She put her finger to her chin, tapping there. "What am I missing?" she mumbled to herself.

Jack, who'd been watching, shrugged. "Maybe the kitchen sink."

She snapped her fingers. "The mixer! I forgot the coke! Can't have a mixed drink without the mixer."

Jack shook his head. "You certainly can't."

And she spun around and opened the fridge removing a small can of coke. With careful hands so as not to overflow the drink, she topped off the glasses with a dainty splash. Then she admired her work. "There. Voila. Enjoy."

She passed the drink to him, then picked up her own. He looked a little reticent but then lifted his glass. "Merry Christmas."

She lifted her glass as well. "And to you."

And she took a big gulp.

The bitter burn hit her first, but it was nothing compared to the retching aftertaste. Alcohol came spewing out of her mouth,, spraying the countertop. Her mouth and eyes screwed shut. "That doesn't.." *Cough.* "Taste…" *Cough.* "How I remember it tasting." She wiped her eyes and patted at her sternum before spotting the darkened sprinkles of liquid on Jack's sleeve. "Ah, I'm so sorry, I got it all over you."

So fucking embarrassing. She swiped a paper towel and began dabbing at Jack's arm, acutely aware of the heft of muscle there. He patted her hand with his. "Hey, don't worry about it. It's an old sweatshirt."

Her dabbing slowed down until she realized his hand was on hers, and then she snatched it away and frowned. "I've failed at making a drink." Just add it to the list of things she'd failed at this year: Keeping a friend. Making a drink. "You'd think I could do something so basic."

"Here…" Jack gently tugged the crumpled paper towel and then the glass out of her fisted hand. "Don't be so hard on yourself. Mixing drinks takes skill just like anything else in the world. And it's not the drink that's wrong. It's just the occasion. Maybe we need to start with something a little less…"

"Disgusting?"

"I was gonna say *elaborate*." He pushed up the sleeves of his grey sweatshirt displaying thick forearms, a vein running along the inner length to his wrist. "Let's keep it simple. Clean. I'll show you. Do you like martinis?"

She crossed her arms over her chest. "Probably not." She'd never ordered one at a bar so she wasn't even sure, but still, she liked the gentle way he was speaking to her. And she didn't hate those forearms either.

He chuckled. "You're honest. I like that." He sorted through her line up of bottles, choosing one. "This is good Vermouth. Bianco. Not too sweet. Not too dry. I think it'll suit your tastes. And this gin…" He sifted through the extra liquor stored in the freezer, lifting the bottle to show her. "Top shelf. We carry it at my restaurant."

"Uncle Joe has high-end preferences."

"Really? I couldn't tell." He said wincing slightly as he pulled the stopper from the bottle with a hollow thunk. "This house is so modest."

"It's not modest at all—" But then she paused, examining the expectant look on his face." — oh, you're joking!" She laughed in an embarrassingly squawk-like way. "I get it, I get what you're saying. You're funny."

"Wet or dry?" Jack set two wide rimmed glasses out in front of him.

She almost choked on her own saliva. "Excuse me?"

"The martini. How'd you like to try it?"

"Oh." She cleared her throat. "You're the expert."

He nodded. "Wet, it is."

August watched with fascination at how quickly and confidently he used his hands. First, he filled a large mixing glass with the ice, the small round balls tumbling excitedly. Then, without measuring he poured from each bottle into the glass. "Does your uncle have a mixing spoon anywhere?"

Without saying anything, August reached forward near

Jack's waist and opened the hidden drawer above the ice fridge where Uncle Joe kept his fancy drinking tools.

"Perfect. Everything I need." He obtained a slender spoon with a long handle and worked the tip into the glass, clinking against the ice, stirring the settled liquid at the bottom. After several stirs, he excised the spoon, and dabbed the small wet end of it to the outside of his hand, near his thumb. His tongue peeked out for only a moment, sampling the spot. His gaze flitted to her. "Mmm. I always like to have a taste."

"Uh huh…" she stuttered, fidgeting with the hem of her shirt. Why was her heart beating so damned hard?

Then he acquired a metal strainer, angling it against the mouth of the mixing glass and tipped it so that each martini glass filled to the brim with a satisfying splash.

"Are most chefs drink experts?" she asked.

He turned to the fridge, grabbed a lemon from the fruit drawer. "The ones who bartended throughout their early twenties are. Olivia and I used to work at the same bar, all those years ago."

He rolled the lemon on the counter and worked off a small peel from the rind with a knife, slicing each side with confident, quick cuts. When he was done, he picked up each peel and turned it rind down above the surface of the drink and squeezed so that aromatic puffs fluttered onto the glass. And then, her eyes widened as he worked the little strip with both hands, his thumb and index finger moving effortlessly, rhythmically, rolling the peels into perfect, singular curls.

As he set the delicate twists into the drink, he gazed up at her, as if he were checking in. She averted her eyes, a cool wave of excitement rushing down her neck, until he turned around again, gathering a few green, tooth-leaved sprigs. He pinched a bit off and let it float on the drink. "And a little mint to keep it festive."

He pushed the drink over the counter towards her, his dark eyes glimmering. "Go on, give it a try."

She took a tentative sip from the wide rim. "Mmmm!" The peppery flavor of juniper and the citrus finish of the lemon stung her lips, but in the most decadent way possible. She knew it was one of those things that was an *acquired* taste but somewhere along the line she must've acquired it. Or maybe she too had Uncle Joe's preference for finer things. She lowered her glass. "This one goes down in all the right ways."

"You said it, not me." And he raised his glass to his lips and then August's world went completely still when over the rim, *he winked at her.*

Oh, my fucking god. She'd been winked at before. But not like that.

She fell speechless, the silence beat between them until she could summon words. "Where..where's Holiday?" The kitten hadn't been in her little enclosure.

The color on his cheeks reddened. "Don't judge me, but she's here." His hand hooked into the pocket of his hoodie, pulling the material to the side and revealing the tiny ears and face of the kitten in the pouch. "Couldn't let her get lonely out there. Nobody likes to sleep by themselves."

Was he flirting with her? Hot men did *not* flirt with her. At least not that she could ever recall. Maybe she hadn't noticed. Cursory alarms sirened in her head.

But also, he seemed so sincere. So caring and sweet.

August's heart clenched in her chest. She'd never really been one for small, sweet creatures, but the combination of the large man and tiny kitten were doing *things* to her. Somewhere deep in her belly, something flickered.

"So…" she mumbled, her thumb windshield-wiping the cold condensation on the glass. She sipped nervously.

"So." He said, mimicking her sip. His voice didn't trail like hers. Didn't seem so unsure.

"I guess now would be a good time to mention that none of the other guests will arrive until tomorrow. At least, I hope they'll make it by tomorrow." But also, she found herself just a bit less concerned about their prompt arrivals now…

He shrugged. "I figured as much."

"You did?"

"I mean, I've been talking to Olivia. She's my friend too."

"Oh, right."

"And I could hear you talking in your room."

Her eyes went wide, her voice a little peep. "Oh… so then you heard me…"

"Call me a himbo? Yeah, I heard that."

August clenched her glass. Her tongue pressed hard against the roof of her mouth. "It's not what you think."

"A himbo isn't a big, silly man?"

"I didn't mean it as an insult." *Although, she had.*

"I might be a chef, but you don't have to sugarcoat things for me if that's how you feel."

She snorted at the corny pun. And while his voice was kind, she stuttered with guilt. "No, no, no, look. A himbo isn't just a big, silly man, he's also excessively handsome." *Oh no.* She squeezed her eyes shut for a moment. Not the save she was going for.

His face was tilted with a little smirk. "You think I'm excessively handsome."

"No, of course not."

"Just regular handsome, then."

"I'm completely neutral towards you." But then, she saw that his mouth pressed into a sheepish grin. "Oh, you're joking again."

"Look, I don't want this to come off as ungrateful for your hospitality, but I get it. I'm a strange man. In your space. Your friends aren't here. I can leave if you want."

She shifted her weight on her feet. Less than an hour ago she would've had him packing his bags, but now she wasn't so sure. "You can't leave. Nobody can leave! Nobody can arrive. Look outside." She gestured to the back wall window which overlooked the now entirely white and foggy sky, the mountains a hazy, dark silhouette in the distance. "A literal blizzard."

"I drive a truck. I'd be fine. I can get out of here in a moment's notice, just say the word."

"I…I want you to stay. I'd feel guilty if you got stranded or something. Even if we're strangers. I'm not completely devoid of emotions. And this martini isn't so bad,"

"You sure?"

She nodded. "Olivia invited you, you're her friend, so the least I can do is lend a hospitable hand." She blushed at her choice of words. Did she want to lend this man a hand or what…*Get your mind out of the gutter.* "Besides, it's not your fault if I seem uncomfortable. Everything makes me uncomfortable."

He set down his glass and then stood in front of her, hands rested on his hips, a thoughtful look on his face. "I have an idea…just, hear me out, okay?"

"Okay."

"Why don't we get to know each other a little bit. Nothing weird, but something fun. To break the ice…that way we won't be perfect strangers."

August was curious. And more than that, she was a little titillated.

Maybe she was a little hard up, too. It'd been at least seven months since she'd slept with anyone. Her last time had been with another accountant at a different firm. They'd met at a conference and talked for several weeks. The sex had been middling at best. Not bad, not good. Not nearly as good as watching Jack lick gin off the side of his hand which had really raised the sexiness bar as far as she was concerned.

"What did you have in mind?" she asked.

"Sit with me." Jack walked over to the small oak table overlooking the window.

She followed, self conscious of how she was walking the

whole time and then pulled out the chair and sat down, crossing her legs. Then she uncrossed them. *No, crossed is better.* And crossed them again.

She was really getting a good look at Jack now. He was tall with a wild thatch of dark brownish-red hair on his head. Almost auburn. He didn't have a beard but by the look of his very dark five-o-clock shadow he was just a few hours away from growing one. His eyes were a deep brown, deep set and framed by thick eyebrows and a strong brow line. His jaw was perfectly cut and highlighted by the dark shadow of his stubble.

She wondered briefly what he might look like without a shirt on.

Then she realized he was waiting for her to speak. "Well, I'm sitting. How do we play this ice breaker game?"

"Rules are simple. You ask me a question, I'll ask you a question. The only stipulation is that the question can't lead to any small talk."

"That's perfect. I hate small talk."

He nodded. "I know, I heard you. I'll start with something easy, though." He tapped his knuckles to the table as if it helped him think. "What's your favorite dessert?"

August snorted a little. "What a strange thing to ask. Nevermind, that's the point." She only had to contemplate for a second. "Crème brûlée. My favorite dessert is crème brûlée. My grandmother used to make it when we were kids. Reminds me of being with family. Is that boring?"

"Not boring. There's actual fire involved. But I think I get it. You like simple, elegant, clean. Like that martini, too."

"Maybe it's because I'm a CPA. I don't like when the ingredients get messy. Always have to have my ducks in a row."

Jack leaned forward, his hands clasped together on the table. "Can I tell you a secret?"

Her eyes went a little wide but she leaned in as well, her curiosity piqued. "Yes."

"I don't know what a CPA is."

She broke out in a real laugh and pointed at him. "Himbo!"

Then he laughed as well, lifting his hands. "Guilty."

"It stands for certified public accountant."

"You work with numbers?"

"Mostly financial planning. That kind of thing."

"So, you're smart."

"Smart but not smart enough to mix a drink."

He chuckled. "Your turn."

She sipped at her martini, the buzz of alcohol easing her normally prickled nerves. She let her curiosity speak for itself. "What's the deal with the kitten? I don't know many men who volunteer at animal shelters. Or have cat supplies in their car."

But it also seemed evident now that she mostly knew all the wrong men anyway.

"Great question. See, you're good at this. Okay, story-time." He rubbed the stem of his glass as he talked. She watched, vaguely mesmerized by the motion. "I used to have a roommate with a cat. Curly Fry was his name. He weighed, like, twenty-three pounds. He wasn't fat though, he was just a big boy. And I'd never had a cat growing up." He rubbed his forearms. "I got so attached. Can't explain it. The little bastard clawed his way into my heart. He would always sleep next to my pillow at night, curled right up under my neck. Thought he might suffocate me, but I'd never move him. Used to make my roommate so mad. We'd laugh and say that Curly Fry was really mine."

"That sounds nice."

Jack scratched the back of his head, then raked his fingers through the front wave of his hair, making it even messier and somehow more attractive. Effortless. It made her think about what that messy hair looked like after sex.

"Yep. It was all good until my roommate got a job in Germany. "

"Oh no."

"Moved out. Took Curly Fry with him."

She winced. "Ouch."

"I didn't think I'd miss him so much—the cat, not the roommate. Didn't realize he would matter to me after the fact. But damn, it was hard. Like losing a best friend."

August nodded at that. "I understand." She knew what it was like to lose a good friend. She shook the thoughts away.

"I was pretty excited to find Holiday. I've missed having a cat around."

"And that's why you volunteer at the animal shelter."

He took a beat before answering. "Yeah, I like the companionship. Always on the lookout for the right one." His heavy gaze lingered on her. "Come to think of it, that was the last time I cried too. I'm not even embarrassed to admit it. I wept like a baby the first night without Curly Fry."

August gave a small smile at his admission. "I bet Curly Fry misses you too."

"There's a good question." He sat back in his chair, legs outstretched. "When's the last time you cried?"

August's face tensed. That was a story she was certainly *not* going to be sharing with a stranger, ice breakers or not. "I can't remember…" she muttered. Blindly, she reached for her drink, taking a sip only to find a mere drop left. She set the glass down and clasped her hands together, a little desperate to change the subject. "Now I feel terrible."

"For what?"

"For giving you a hard time about bringing that kitten in here. She's cute, I'll admit it."

"She's real cute."

"Can I see her?"

"Of course, she's right here." He gestured to the lower half of his shirt.

"Yes, but can I hold her?" Jack made it look so nice the way he cupped Holiday to his chest.

"Sure. Hey, little thing. Let's get you out of this pouch for a minute," Jack murmured as he reached into his sweatshirt, the kitten's legs splaying out, the sound of tiny claws unclenching from the warmth of the pouch. He motioned for August to come closer. "C'mere. I don't wanna pass her over the table. She's still a little scared."

August scooted her chair with little bumpy hops until she was right beside Jack, a physical warmth emanating from such close proximity, the soft scent of pine drifting to her nose.

She'd never held a kitten before. Hesitantly, she reached out her hand, and right before she made contact—

Kheeeee!

She jerked away. "Why'd she do that? She hissed at me!"

Jack chuckled letting Holiday climb down his shirt and back into her little pouch. "Animals can tell when you're unsure of yourself. You've got to be confident with your approach. Here, I'll show you. Put your hand out."

"Put my hand out?"

"For a demonstration."

"Okay," she said hesitantly but still stretched her fingers and palm upwards.

"See, you're coming at her like this." He brought his fingers towards her palm but then jerked back a little, then pushed forward again, his hand shaking and hesitant.

She laughed at how spot on his impression was, and suddenly she could picture the situation very clearly. She must've made the kitten nervous. "Right, I get it. She doesn't know me, and my approach didn't inspire trust."

"Bingo. See, you understand better than you think." Jack bent forward ever so slightly, but his movement made her catch her breath. It took everything in her to pay attention to his words. "The way to approach Holiday is like this," he explained. Then with a gentle but firm touch, he cupped the underside of her hand with his own.

She watched as his other hand traveled towards her palm in what felt like slow motion. With slight pressure, he pressed the tip of his index and middle finger to the center of her palm. Her pulse raced wildly. Then he dragged it down the dip of her hand all the way to the ridged and sensitive thin skin of her wrist. Slowly, his fingers drifted away leaving a trail of tingling skin in their wake. "Does that inspire your trust?" His voice fell hushed.

They locked eyes. She couldn't look away this time.

He leaned forward at exactly the same time she did, their foreheads clumsily colliding. "Shit, I'm so sorry." Her hand flew to her forehead rubbing the spot, but then they were still inches away, his breath against her mouth.

Slowly she pushed her face forward, closer to his, until their mouths were a centimeter from touching. "Should we?"

"Shit. Yeah…" he whispered. And then their mouths were touching, brushing against each other. Her eyes fluttered shut, stuck on the brink of a kiss. She couldn't even believe she'd gotten this far. They were both breathing hard now. And she felt his hand reach the side of her ribcage, fingertips gliding up and down the sensitive area.

Mrow! Mrrrooww!

The sound came from Jack's sweatshirt.

She scrunched her nose, squeezed her eyes even tighter, but they couldn't ignore it.

Mrrrroooowww!

"I think Holiday needs a nap…" Jack whispered against her mouth. "I'm gonna put her in her pen."

She opened her eyes, nodding. "I understand," she said in a haze.

He broke away, cool air caressing her skin where his hot mouth had been. She didn't follow him into the living room, just watched his silhouette disappear around the corner. Her heart was racing now and a fluttery elation shot through her.

She barely knew this man. But she *liked* him.

She didn't have time to text Olivia or Elliot for advice. She'd have to make her own decisions about how to act. Besides, Olivia would say something like, "Oh my god, *Jack?* You should totally sleep with Jack. I love Jack. Maybe you'll marry Jack! I'm your maid of honor, don't you fucking forget it."

And Elliot would say something like, "Fuck his brains out, it's Christmas. Give the gift of a big, old, fat O for the holidays."

She squeezed her thighs together, small slivers of erotic pressure shooting up to her abdomen.

So, what was stopping her exactly?

Chapter 4

Jack's footsteps returned before she could question herself, and this time she regarded him beneath her eyelashes. He paused in the threshold of the doorway, one hand on the doorframe, as if he was awaiting invitation.

She bit her lip, and leaned back, getting another good look at him. He was tall but his body had a graceful and lean ease about it. The divet of muscle on his shoulders showed through his grey sweatshirt. His jeans fit him well, highlighting how long his legs were. She was a tall woman, but even still, he was much taller. She didn't often date men taller than her, and she had to admit she kind of liked it.

One hot man and all the feminism leaves your body, huh?

"Are you coming back?" She tucked a brown curl behind her ear, feeling excited but self conscious.

He didn't say anything, just stalked towards her slowly, an intense energy radiating from his gaze.

What would he do? Her clit throbbed in anticipation. She wasn't used to this build up.

"You want me to, right?" He asked.

She could only manage a nod.

"That's all I needed to know." He rounded the chair next

to her and pulled it out with a jerk, then reclined, sitting face to face with her. His hand made contact with the vulnerable skin of her neck brushing away her errant strands of hair. Then she shivered as he traced the line from her shoulder to her collarbone. At this point, she was panting, her skin ablaze.

"What are you doing?" she whispered.

"Nothing you can't stop at any moment. Would you like me to stop?"

"No…" the word came out strained and the pad of his rough finger traveled to her other collarbone, then back up the side of the column of her neck and around the shell of her ear. She let out an exhale, leaning her head, nuzzling at nothing from the touch.

"Are you going to kiss me?"

"Shhh…" This time he brought his finger to her lips, first to shush her and then to trace the line of them until he pinched her chin, tilting her face down. "Ask me to do it."

Embarrassment flared in her chest. "What?"

He was looking her dead in the eye now. "Ask me to kiss you."

"But why?"

"Because I like it when a woman tells me exactly what she wants." He raised his chin. A challenge.

"I thought you were …" She searched hard trying to come up with words, too mesmerized by his closeness. "A nice guy."

His other hand came to the back of her head, gently fisting her hair at the root, her head jerking ever so slightly back from his grasp. She audibly gasped. It didn't hurt. It felt *amazing.* She wasn't expecting it either, but the surprise made it feel so good.

"I am a nice guy." His voice vibrated against her. "But not all the time."

Tingles raced up her spine. No man had *ever* spoken to her this way.

Fuck her dignity. Fuck embarrassment. Fuck her awkwardness. She wanted this. "Do it, now. Kiss me," she whispered.

"I want to hear you say *please, Jack*."

"Please…Jack…"

He released his grasp on the back of her head, his hand coming to cup her jaw. He eased her head to the side exposing the long line of her neck. Instead of her lips, his mouth and tongue found the taut skin there, goosebumps rippling everywhere from the mere press of his tongue.

His mouth traveled up the column all the way to the side of her jaw and finally, then finally met her mouth in a shared inhale. He licked at the seam of her lips and she opened for him, allowing their tongues to touch, but only for a second until he pulled away.

Still, electric.

She sagged in her chair as if she'd been drugged but in the best possible way. But also, why'd he stop?

"That's…" she swallowed hard. "That's it?"

His gaze was smoldering. His face flushed belying any indifference he might have towards the kiss. "Up to you. Tell me what you want next."

"Do it again." She cleared her throat. "But more. Do it more." No embarrassment this time. She was too far gone in the moment. He could ask her to bark like a dog and she'd get on all fours and howl at the moon.

This time, his hands slithered up her knees to her thighs. He nodded slightly. "Get off that chair."

"And sit where?"

"My lap."

"Oh." She'd barely risen when his hands grabbed her on either side of her hips. Blunt fingertips pressed into the rounded flesh. He pulled her on top of him, guiding one leg to wrap around his waist at a time.

That's when she felt it. His hard cock pressed against her crotch. It did things to her she didn't expect. She barely knew this man, but he'd made her feel more comfortable in minutes than anyone she'd ever been with. Instinctively, she rolled her hips so that she could rub her clit against him, and a small pang of pleasure shot from her pelvis all the way down, curling her toes in her snowflake Christmas socks.

He let out a small groan. "God, we're not even naked, and you're already riding my dick so good." He bucked his hips once pushing his erection into her. She bounced with the motion and moaned, her eyes rolling back into her head. She rocked into him again and again until he got the hint and they were rubbing against each other in unison.

"Kiss me again," she said, her eyes fluttering open. This time she knew to tell him. Knew that he listened when she gave directives.

His gaze went dark but he complied, threading his fingers into the hair at the back of her nape and drawing her lips near, catching her mouth in another kiss.

His tongue brushed against hers and she opened her mouth wider, as her hips rolled, vocal cords vibrating and sending electrical sparks shooting from their joined spot. Little involuntary muffled gasps escaped from her mouth.

As they kissed, her hands snaked up the front of his chest, feeling the hardness of his muscles. This man was solid as a rock, but his sweatshirt was a direct contrast, both soft and warm. Then she wrapped her arms around his neck pressing herself so close there was barely room for air between their bodies.

He broke from the kiss, his lips traveled to her ear, his tongue flicking so lightly at the outer shell of skin there. "I think you're beautiful..." he said, his voice was soft, causing painful goosebumps to ripple down the side of her face and head, she could feel it everywhere, even in her pussy. Another lick at her ear. "As soon as I saw you I wanted to kiss you."

"I find that hard to believe," she muttered, but she was barely even aware she had spoken.

He pulled back with an incredulous look on her face. And then it dawned on her how ridiculous that statement was to say to a man who was currently kissing her. She snorted. "Sorry. Just forget what I said. Kiss me more, kiss me more." And he did.

His scent surrounded her, and she breathed in big, trying to get another whiff of him, his smell so intoxicating. "What kind of detergent do you use?" She said between kisses. "Your sweatshirt smells so good."

Her hands traveled down to his shoulders and around his arms, down to the hem of his shirt where they gently played with the material.

"I don't know," he answered.

Emboldened, she tugged at the soft edge. "I want you to take it off. Now. Hurry."

"Yes, ma'am." He reached behind his neck and yanked the grey material over his head, struggling to get out of the shirt fast enough, his face flushed and his hair was wild when he emerged. He flung it to the floor, and she gave herself a second to take him in as the hard planes of his chest, the divots in his wide shoulders, the dark hair trailing down from his belly button came into view.

"Holy shit," she whispered.

"And you can do whatever you want with me."

Oh, shit. This was exciting. Even Elliot would think so.

"Really?" She ran her fingernails from his waistband to his belly button, his abs muscles flexed in response. He groaned quietly, his head falling back. Encouraged, she explored further, letting her hands roam up the hot but silky skin. "I never do anything like this."

His voice strained. "Well, you're doing a good job."

Without even meaning to, her lips curled up at the corner. She wasn't ready for him to touch her down there. She was tempted, but her nerves would surely stop her from being able to...*open up*. She liked him, but what if everything went horribly wrong? What if she didn't like him after he touched her like that?

But...but she was still very turned on.

Maybe she could just touch him. She could see *his* body instead. What were the odds she could give him an orgasm that would have him wanting more? Give her time to warm up to bigger things. She was good at following directives as well. She could learn what he liked.

She patted his leg. "Take your pants off too."

He raised his eyebrows. "Yes, ma'am."

"If..." she stuttered. "If that's okay with you."

He leaned back in the chair, putting space between their upper bodies and undid the top button of his jeans and then worked the zipper down as well. "Lift up a bit..." he muttered as he attempted to wiggle the waistband past his hips. She went to stand but his hands came hard on her hips.

"Don't *leave*," he growled. "Just give a little space. But *don't* leave. Don't even think about it."

She paused. "Fine." She lifted up on her thighs to offer a small gap between them so he could get his pants down past his hips. The view of his navy boxer briefs housing his enormous erection was now directly in her line of vision. She licked her lips, blushing when she looked back up at him. He gave her a knowing look.

His hands grabbed her hips and forced her back on his lap, the soft material of his boxer briefs and hardness of his erection pressing against her crotch. He rolled his hips again, hands squeezing her flesh, eyes on her. "C'mon then," he encouraged. "Do what you want with me."

"You mean it?"

He grabbed her neck, yanking her to him. His kiss was no longer subtle, it was urgent, sloppy, their mouths opened wide and their tongues lashing recklessly. Little mewling sounds came from her diaphragm that she didn't even recognize as her own. The single line of pleasure emanating from the connected space between them began to undulate, stretching and contracting throughout her body. Could she come this way?

She had never come with a man before. Only by herself or with her vibrator. She hadn't expected...well, she hadn't expected any of this.

She pulled away. She couldn't. She couldn't let herself go this way with a man she barely knew. Even if he was...well, whatever it was that he was. His naked chest was heaving, and he glared at her, his mouth slightly parted. "Well?" He said, the word gruff.

Without thinking about it, her hands went to the waistband of his boxer briefs, yanking them down and revealing the heft of his cock. She touched the silky skin with her fingertips and found it hot to the touch. His eyes shuttered closed, arms falling to his side. She leaned forward and kissed him on the lips, the touch lingering for a moment, his head lifting to chase her lips when she once again drew away.

Then, she grabbed his hand, uncurling his fist from the side of the chair. As she flattened it, palm facing her, an idea blossomed in her brain.

She wanted him to think that she knew what she was doing, even though she didn't. So, maybe she could find a way to work this to her advantage.

"What's next..." he asked, but his voice trailed off when she brought his palm to her mouth and she licked it from the base to fingertip. "Mmmm..." he groaned, licking his lips.

"You're going to show me how to do this," she said. She lifted his cock and wrapped his hand around the shaft, her own hands wrapped around his fist. Slowly, she guided him, pulling his grip up the shaft all the way to the head, where she leaned over and spit on the head, then rubbed it in with the fingertips of her free hand. Lubrication was always the first rule, that much she knew. He groaned audibly.

"We're going to do it together," she said.

"Fuck, you're gonna kill me."

She nodded hesitantly, and they both began to stroke his hard length. His hand moving up and down, hers moving with it, occasionally catching the parts of his naked skin that he wasn't. He was large enough that she had to use both hands.

He pulled her in for a kiss as they jerked him off together, wet and hot. He wouldn't let her move from his grasp, so she stayed there. Their hands between them working hard, and their mouths connected, lazy tongues occasionally lashing out to lick.

She followed his lead when his stroking quickened in tempo, the sound of rubbing skin and their own breathing the only thing resonating between them. "Yes, yes...yes..." he murmured against her. "Fuck, this is hot."

When his kissing became distracted, more erratic, she knew he was nearing the edge. She kept up with his hand as it flew up and down. Her whole body bounced with the rhythm on top of him, his hand squeezing her ass. Then when he broke away from the kiss as his eyes shut and his head dropped back, she knew it would happen soon. "I'm coming..." he said, his words a strained whisper. He kissed her again. *"Fuck, pull up your shirt."*

It took a second for the words to register. She was so wrapped up in their activities, but hastily she grabbed the hem of her shit when the words finally resonated. "Oh!"

He yanked it messily over her breasts which were still covered with a sensible black bra. His free hand grasped onto one of the cups and shoved it down harshly, exposing her hardened nipples to the hot air between them.

"You wanna come on them?" she asked, proud of her own fearlessness.

"Yeah...yes. Please." He nodded, urgently. "Let me come all over them, I wanna be dripping off your nipples..." he said, his body tensing.

Her pussy gushed, the space between her thighs going

slick. She leaned forward, jerking him off in earnest, this time with her tits hanging directly over his dick, their hands pumping away. She might've laughed at how awkwardly she was bent over if she wasn't so fucking turned on.

Within moments, hot ropes of white come slashed across her one breast while another rope dripped from the slope of her other breast.

His head fell back on the chair, his arms slack at his side. Inwardly, she was glowing. She didn't know she was capable of doing something like that. It was such a small thing but somehow…so dirty.

"Whoa," he said.

"Yeah, whoa." Slowly, she lifted her leg to get off his lap and wipe the jizz off her. Had she ever let a man come on her breasts before?

Quite literally never.

"Don't get up…" he murmured.

"I gotta clean this off me."

"Leave it there. It's my turn."

Leave it there? His turn? She was considering it when a loud, stressed meow came from the other room.

"Holiday…" he groaned. "Timing couldn't be worse."

"You should check on her."

This time he let her stand and remove herself from his lap, giving her a double tap on the ass as she straightened out her legs.

She spun around, swiping a paper towel from the counter and wetting it in the sink before cleaning the sticky come from her skin. She wiggled the cups of her bra back up and the hem of her shirt back down, smoothing the fabric with her palms before turning around. Her skin was about a thousand degrees beneath her jeans.

Jack was still indisposed on the chair, but he wiped his forehead with the back of his hand, inhaled once and yanked his boxer briefs and jeans back over his hips. He didn't bother zipping or buttoning them. "I'll be right back. Don't go anywhere."

"Where would I go?"

He softened his tone. "I just mean, stay put so we can focus on you next." He left to check on Holiday.

She didn't actually want him to return the favor. She was too scared of the idea of having an orgasm in front of another person. How very...vulnerable. How did other people do it?

But she didn't want to go anywhere either.

Nervously, she grabbed the gin on the counter and took a swig, wiping her mouth with her sleeve.

After all that, she needed another drink.

His footsteps alerted her of his return and she straightened her spine, her heart rate increasing steadily with anticipation.

Of course, the sight of him was a Christmas present in and of itself. Jesus Christ, he was a good looking man. His hair was a mess now but it suited him with the rough stubble along his face. And his eyelashes were so long and beautiful.

Her fingertips fluttered to her own eyelashes, much shorter and more delicate than his.

He walked to her, pressing her backside against the counter.

"So..." he said, their feet creating a box between them. A new intimacy bloomed. Now, they'd subscribed to a culture of touching. A barrier broken. She wanted to touch him. And he wanted to touch her. He *was* touching her. The fronts of his thighs pressed into hers, he ran his fingers down her upper arms all the way to her hands, lacing them together. "Tell me how you want to come."

"I, umm..." *Shit.* She should've been prepared, but she was absolutely not prepared. What was that allegory people always said—there were two wolves inside of a person? She definitely had two wolves, one that said she should let him give her an orgasm and another that said she should run out of sheer nerves. Which one would she feed? "Are you hungry?" she croaked.

He gave her a darkened look. "Yes, very," he whispered directly into her ears, making her nipples harden to aching points.

Shit. She put her hands on his chest to push him away but he caught her by the wrists and guided her hands up to his neck. "Get up on the counter and I'll show you just how much I can eat."

The glint in his eye was so compelling she almost did exactly what she was told, but...

You don't even know this guy.

You've never done this before.

You just jerked off a stranger in the middle of your uncle's kitchen.

You let him come on your boobs!

Was this the Christmas Spirit everyone was always talking about?

She ducked her head and stepped away from him. "It's a nice offer, but I'm going to decline for now."

He raised his eyebrows as if he was surprised. "Oh?"

"Sorry, are you angry?"

He ran his hands through his thick, dark hair. "Of course not. I just thought maybe you'd be interested after we..."

"It's not that I'm not interested, per say, it's just..."

"You have a boyfriend?"

She covered her mouth to muffle the snort that came out of her. *A boyfriend?* Please. She hadn't had a boyfriend since seventh grade. Her first and only. "Don't be ridiculous."

"Did I do something wrong?"

"Well, you showed up three hours early with a stray kitten."

He nodded, considering that. "True. But I meant the other stuff."

She nibbled on her lip. "If I have to be honest..."

"Yes, always be honest."

She squirmed, as if working the words from her brain to

her mouth. "We're moving at a faster pace than I'm accustomed. Maybe you're a little more used to it than me. This kind of thing, that is."

"I see. I get it."

"You do?" she asked skeptically.

"What would I get out of making you do something you don't want to do? Nothing good."

She smiled slightly. "You make a valid point."

He smiled back. "Then we're on the same page."

She felt fidgety under his gaze, so she pulled out her phone to stare at anything else.

She had several text messages from her friends. She held up her phone. "I'm gonna check in with the girls."

He nodded and she shuffled off to the living room, leaning against the overstuffed leather couch as she read her messages.

Olivia: How's hot Jack doing? You hanging in there?

Elliot: Don't forget to check behind the medicine cabinet for prescription drugs! You never know what you might find. I would send you my edibles via text message if I could, but right now they're in my checked luggage.

She texted back quickly. *I gave Jack a hand job in the kitchen!!! What do I do now?!*

Olivia: Huh???

Elliot: Thatta girl. He better return the favor.

August: But what do I do now?

Olivia: Oh! Oh! I know! Ask him to make you a grilled cheese. They're his specialty. His restaurant is elevated comfort food.

August: What does that have to do with anything?

Olivia: I dunno, I just like to eat after sex.

Elliot: Sometimes I like to eat before.

At first August was frustrated at the lack of advice, but then she creeped back into the kitchen, finding Jack checking his own phone at the table. He lifted his gaze at her entrance.

"What if I told you I was hungry?" she said.

Chapter 5

GRILLED CHEESE WAS INDEED JACK'S SPECIALTY. BUT NOT JUST any grilled cheese. Jack set a plate before her with a thick, gooey sandwich finished to a beautiful, greasy golden crisp. "Goat cheese and mozzarella with sliced plum tomatoes fried in Irish Butter on a thick cut brioche." He sliced the sandwich in half right there, the knife making a satisfying crunch sound and then rocked the knife back and forth until the two halves parted.

"Wow, I just use white bread with that sliced cheese that comes individually wrapped in plastic."

"Ain't nothing wrong with that." Then he retrieved a small mason jar from the counter and a spoon. "The final touch."

"Wait! What's that?"

"My specialty. Hot chili honey."

"I've never had honey on a grilled cheese before." The variations on cheese and tomato she could handle, but she was skeptical about the rest. On the other hand, he *had* made her a great drink. "You know what? I trust you."

Jack twisted open the lid and dipped his spoon in, then with the flourish of a professional chef, he drizzled the honey on top of her sandwich, zig zags of golden amber. "Take a bite. If you don't like it, you can have mine. But something tells me you'll like it."

August brought the sandwich to her lips and took the first bite. "Ohmygod," she said, quickly covering her full mouth with the flat of her hand while she chewed. The flavors were both subtle and vibrant. The sweetness of the honey paired perfectly with the smooth but earthy flavors of the cheese, and then a bite of heat at the end gave the little extra kick it needed to stay exciting. She swallowed. "This is the best thing I've ever eaten."

Jack drizzled honey on his sandwich and bit in as well. "Thank you."

She took another bite. "Elevated comfort food." She got it now.

"That's right."

They ate in an amicable silence. While she relished the sandwich, August reflected on what she'd done, incredulous by her own action. And there was something fascinating to her about the situation they'd found themselves in. How she'd essentially assisted him in jerking off his own cock, but now they were sitting there together licking sweet grease from their fingers like nothing at all had happened. She was thankful for the comfort, given that it was just the two of them.

August checked the weather on her phone: *record inches of snowfall for at least the next twelve hours*. They were now completely snowed in. No one was getting in. No one was getting out. Luckily all her friends were safe. Olivia and her brother had managed to get a room at a hotel. Elliot was warm and cozy at the airport in some kind of first class lounge somewhere. So, at the very least she didn't have to worry about them.

And luckily they still had power because if the electricity went out, they'd really be screwed. It was twenty degrees outside and dropping, and August *needed* the distraction of her phone.

Much too soon, August's sandwich was gone. She swirled her fingertip onto the ceramic surface of the plate, mopping up crumbs and licking them off.

"I can make more if you're still hungry."

She didn't want more food though. Now, she wanted more of something else. She could feel a shift in her level of comfort. It was happening more quickly with Jack than it ever happened with anyone. Maybe some people just had the magic touch?

She shifted in her seat, her thighs still slick from their activities before and now her hands were greasy from the grilled cheese. Reflexively she pushed her chair out, the wood scraping against the floor. If they were going to fuck—*Oh my god, was she ready for something like that?*—she needed to shave her legs and clean up her body. "I have to take a shower," she blurted out.

"Think I could probably wash up as well." His tone didn't betray any motives, but nevertheless, her nerves sparked.

"Bye." She stood up stiffly and shuffled out of the kitchen, practically running up the stairs to her bedroom.

When she reached the solitude of the bathroom, she caught her breath.

Time to gameplan. Time to prepare. For what? She wasn't even sure.

The shower in the master bathroom was upright and surrounded by glass, and immediately steamed up when she turned on the hot water.

Luckily, she had packed a fresh razor which she removed from the package and went to town on her weeks worth of growth on her legs and pubic region. She didn't go full Brazilian the way Elliot did, but she also didn't dye her pubes hot pink like Olivia. She was somewhere in between.

In her haze, as she slid the razor up her leg, she felt an uncharacteristic sting. *Ouch.* Then before she could look away, a tiny red pool began welling up on her shin bone, the blood coming out faster than the water could wash it away. Oh shit.

Don't faint. Don't faint.

August squeezed her eyes shut. The sight of blood dizzied her balance. She futilely grasped at the wet tiled wall. Oh god, the world was getting smaller. She pushed the handle down and stumbled out of the shower, pulling her towel off the hook and wrapping It around her.

This wasn't good. She needed help. The cold air hit her hard, but it wasn't enough to stop the panic.

Don't look, don't look, don't look.

She grabbed onto the inner handle of the glass door but miscalculated her aim and before she knew it, she was flat on the ground. The shock of the fall rendering her frozen.

A second passed by and then—

Thump!

Her entire shower caddy fell off the top ledge where she'd suctioned it to the wall, falling right onto her foot.

"*Shit! Fuck!*" She covered her mouth with her hand, face screwed up hard at the wild shock of pain from both her fall and the shower caddy. "Goddammit."

The sound of footsteps came only a moment later.

Jack busted through the door before she could even sit up. A huge gush of relief. She didn't even give a fuck that she was in nothing but a towel. "Blood..." she panted, belly flat against the cold bathroom tile, legs bent and splayed with a shower caddy and all its contents unearthed around her foot.

"Blood?"

She couldn't make out his face in the steam of the bathroom, but he was clearly alarmed. And before she knew it, he was wrapping her towel around her and hoisting her up over his shoulder like she was a sack of potatoes.

"What're you doing!" she screamed.

He set her back on the bed, more gently this time. He was

panting as he barked out, "You said blood, but I couldn't see anything. Where's the blood? Are you okay?"

She daintily lifted her leg, her toe pointed, head turned away. "I can't look."

"What?" He handled her foot at the heel turning it each and every direction. "I don't see anything, is the bleeding internal? What are you talking about."

She lifted up on her elbows and pointed at the small red knick on her shin. "Thi-this."

He rubbed his thumb back and forth over the vertical shin bone, but the knick was so small that it wasn't even bleeding anymore.

"I have a phobia."

He smiled, but shook his head, gently placing her leg back on the mattress. "Would you like me to kiss it and make it better?"

She pouted. "Phobias are serious."

He grabbed her hand, lacing it together with his. She gave him an incredulous look. "Give me a little squeeze whenever you feel light headed and I'll get you all fixed up." He gave her a little squeeze. She squeezed back, peeking through one eye.

"Fine," she said, but she had her skepticism.

Then very gently he peeled off the layers of a bandaid he'd retrieved from the medicine cabinet while she watched him. When the adhesive touched her skin she inhaled sharply, but he squeezed her hand. Her breath caught, but before she let the black spots overwhelm her vision. She squeezed back.

And amazingly, it worked. She was still conscious!

"Fine, you can do what you said before…"

"What did I say before?"

"You know what?"

"Use your words," his eyes reflected a naughty glint.

"Kiss it? Please."

"You want me to kiss your cut?"

She lifted her leg, toe pointed. "If it'll help."

She opened her eyes to find him kneeling in front of her. Suddenly, now calmed from the sight of blood, the tension grew between them. The realization that she was in a towel and nothing else, and he was fully clothed kneeling before her was so very apparent. Her skin was still damp, and she smelled like peppermint body wash. Her pussy was throbbing again, dammit. Always betraying her at every turn.

"Or would you like me to kiss something else?"

Now that she was already in a vulnerable position, maybe it felt a little easier to be vulnerable. Maybe.

As if he got the telepathic message, his hands crept up to her knees, rubbing the sensitive skin beneath with his calloused thumb. Something about that was so primal that it caused a feeling inside her belly to stir.

He lifted an eyebrow, as if giving her signal, and then his hand glided over her knees and into the crevice between them, moving to the very vulnerable skin of her inner thigh. She held her towel at her chest, watching him closely. He moved slowly, glancing at her as if to check her comfort each time his hand traveled further and further up. Inch by inch.

Her pussy clenched. She'd never been this turned on before.

He parted her thighs slowly but firmly, until she felt the cool air inside her towel. Reflexively, she slammed her legs shut.

He dropped his hands immediately. "I'm so sorry, I thought you wanted me to—"

She scratched the top of her wet head, wincing. "I do, I do, I do..."

"But?"

"Have you ever just been a little …afraid? Just a tiny little bit?"

He furrowed his brow. "Have you never done this with a man before?"

"Depends on what you mean by *this*?"

"Has a man ever made you come before?"

"No."

"Has anyone?"

"Just myself."

"Ah, well that's good. That's good."

"It is?"

"Because then you can teach me."

She considered that. "I'm good at directions. Both giving and getting."

"Good."

She sighed. "But there's another problem."

"Okay."

"Don't judge." She winced, trying to explain her feelings. " I can't watch, but I won't be able to keep my eyes closed. I'll just stare at what you're doing and freak myself out."

He chuckled softly. "I see, so it's the visuals that throw you off."

"Just because…this is new to me."

He thought for a moment. "Maybe we try something out of the box. Take the pressure off a bit. But you've got to be… open to it."

She raised a brow. "What do you mean?"

"Would you like me to show you? You'll have to trust me, but just know I'll stop at any time.

His expression was gentle, she felt no pressure at all. So, she nodded. "I am amenable to this idea."

"Good." He nudged her legs. "Now face the headboard and get on your hands and knees."

Her eyes went big, but she tried to hide her surprise. This might've been one of those times when he wasn't a *nice guy*. "What do I do with the towel?"

"You can keep it on or take it off, but I'm gonna be pulling it up so that I can see you."

She squeezed it extra tight around her ribcage. "I think I'll keep it on for now."

47

"You can always take it off later if you want. The only rule is that it has to feel right."

"Will you take off anything?"

"Do you want me to?"

Yes. "Not…yet."

He leaned in at her side, his breath against her ear. "Anytime you want me to strip naked for you, just say the word."

"Hoooookay."

Then he clapped his hands together which made her jerk in place. He was hot. So hot.

But she was scared.

And excited.

Maybe all she needed was a safe place to hold her vulnerabilities. And while that wasn't the kind of Christmas gift she'd expected this year, it was beginning to feel like it was the one she needed most.

"Well?" he said. His voice was playful now. She felt a weird sensation coming over her. For the first time ever, she was going to trust that someone else would take control of things.

Primly, she straightened out her towel, made sure it was tucked in tight before getting to her hands and knees on the bed, her gaze facing the wall, Jack now behind her. Her heart raced.

"Don't think about me, just think about you. You don't have to see a thing. All you have to do is be. Got it?"

"Got it."

And then, she felt it. The soft breath from his mouth at her thighs. She clenched when she heard his deep inhale and then a groan. He was going to go down on her from behind? Her eyes went wide when she felt his tongue at the folds of her pussy, featherlight, so light she started to giggle. *Flick, flick, flick.* She could barely stand it.

She thought she'd had too much when his tongue traveled north to her ass crack. Thank god she'd just showered. Small Christmas miracles, thank you, Santa. Gently, he slid his tongue up and down until it landed square in the middle of her, flicking back and forth and applying just a small amount of pressure.

"Oh my god…" she breathed.

"You like my tongue on your pretty little asshole, just like this?" he asked in between breaths.

Not always a nice guy.

Before she could even get out a response, his hand had reached around to her pussy, finding her clit. Wetness covered her so when he began to rub slow, big circles all over her, she let out a tiny choking mewl.

Overwhelming sensations flooded her entire body, and she could already feel the inklings of an orgasm building in the pit of her stomach. When she realized it, her body stiffened. Her knuckles whitened as she fisted the sheet.

"You good?" Jack's voice came behind her, his hand slowing. "Just say the word if you need me to stop."

She inhaled deeply. Although warning bells were going off in her head, knowing she held the power to stop him at any time gave her the strength to continue. Because, afterall, she wanted this. *Wow did she want this.* And at this point, she'd do anything to get it, including letting a man she barely knew lick her asshole from behind.

She hadn't even known it was a thing people did! "Keep going, keep going…" she said, with a wiggle of her hips.

He listened, burying his mouth against her, his calloused fingertips easily gliding around her clit. She strained her body now, rolled her hips in a circle so that she could move with the sensation.

She was on a precipice but also so far away, it was the most acute torture she'd ever known, like only getting one good scratch at a still itchy mosquito bite or having to sneeze but not being able to expel one.

She was so frustrated, she forgot to be nervous. "Do it harder!" she bit out, unabashedly.

49

"My hand?" he asked.

"Yes, more pressure, and faster. And…and…keep doing that thing with your mouth. Don't stop, okay?"

"Yes, ma'am." He continued with the motion, her entire ass and pussy soaked now, the moisture being swiped around her in an existential pleasure storm. One she didn't want to wake from.

He pushed harder against her clit, his hand going faster. For a moment she worried his tongue and hand might be getting tired, but then she remembered his words, that she shouldn't think about him at all, that she should only think about the feeling swelling within her—

"Fuck I'm coming…" She said, a guttural moan emanating as her whole body tightened like a string. As long as he didn't change one goddamn thing, this was about to be the orgasm of a lifetime.

The swell of feelings caught and then bloomed inside her, swimming from her clit up her stomach and throughout her fingertips, then down her thighs. She curled her toes, clenched her legs. She was bucking up against him like a wild woman, shameless and hellbent on her own pleasure. She rubbed against him in every which way she possibly could. And then the feeling crested hard and sharp in the center of her stomach and she almost collapsed. Finally ending in a soft floaty feeling.

"Okay, okay, okay…." she let her head fall to the mattress, her ass still exposed and in the air, the coldness around her contrasting with the hot wetness of her body. He gave her one final lick and then let her go. Her whole body dropped to the mattress. She rolled on her back, her hand across her forehead, the bottom half of her towel folded open, but who could possibly give a fuck at a moment like this?

He crawled up on the bed and lay down next to her, his cheek against the pillow. She let her head loll over to look at him. "Wow," was the only thing she could muster.

He laughed, rubbing his eyes. Maybe he was tired after all the work he put in. She laughed too, but she didn't know what she was laughing at. She'd done it. She'd been vulnerable with another person, and he'd taken that seriously, and *look what had happened*.

"Give me a moment," he said. He got up, and she heard the water turn on down the hall. moments of silence passed. Then he returned to the bedroom. "Holiday's all good. Checked on her."

When he laid back down next to her she could also smell the pepperminty notes of toothpaste. So, he'd also brushed his teeth.

Even though she had a towel, she snatched the fluffy white down comforter that was folded over the middle of the bed and yanked it over her shoulder, covering her mostly naked form. Jack followed suit, burrowing beneath the blanket, his hands coming to her waist and drawing her against his warm contour. August felt acutely close to him. More so than she'd felt to anyone for months. And it had been a few rough months, hadn't it?

Before she could stop them, words tumbled from her lips. "Three months ago."

Jack nuzzled her neck. "Three months ago?"

"Three months ago was the last time I cried."

"Oh. I see. What happened?"

"It's a pretty fucked up story, actually."

"Well, now I'm intrigued."

August laughed softly. "Okay, so maybe we don't know each other that well, but I'm sure you've noticed that I don't possess the…warmest of dispositions. It can be difficult for me to make new friends, I won't deny it. I'm lucky to have Olivia and Elliot."

"Olivia's said all good stuff about you."

"Yeah, well, Olivia likes everyone. So, here's the truth. The whole story. The firm where I work…I wouldn't describe it as the friendliest place. I struggled, like really struggled, to connect with my coworkers, and I really hated working there for the longest time. Even on days I was working from home. Until the day they hired my new boss. Another woman. The firm is primarily men, so she was like a beacon of light. And she was such a generous, thoughtful person. The kind of person I really, really looked up to. Trusted. Wanted to be like. She made me feel like I was really talented and worthy. I actually looked forward to my days in the office when she was there. I'd never felt that way at a workplace before. It was just, really nice." She paused to collect her thoughts. Sometimes retelling events felt like reliving her trauma, but she realized she really did want to share this part of herself with Jack. There was a freedom in telling your truth, even if it hurt.

He gave her hip an encouraging squeeze so she kept talking. She might as well spit it out. "Which is why I was very confused one night when I was reviewing an account of mine, and I noticed something was off. The numbers didn't quite add up. And as you know, I like to keep my business in line. When I took it to her, she explained that there was an error and that she would fix it. She was so unphased that I didn't think twice about it. Until I found *another* error the next week. Same thing happened again. Took it to my boss, she told me *don't worry about it.* But this time, I was worried about it. I kept digging…something just didn't sit right with me. And well, it turned out something wasn't right. She had been embezzling hundreds of thousands of dollars from clients and had been doing so for months."

"Oh, shit." Jack's blunt expression almost made her laugh.

"But that's not even the biggest problem. Because here's the god-awful truth about me." She sighed, holding onto the strong forearms now encircled around her ribcage. "I almost didn't turn her in. I really almost didn't do it. I know it sounds ridiculous, because of course I had to turn her in! What she was doing was dishonest and wrong and threatened the livelihoods of everyone around her. But…*but* there was this part of me that just wanted to hold onto to her. The friendship we had. The mentorship. The connection I'd built. I would've risked everything and everyone just for a little warmth from her. But in the end, I knew what I had to do. I still wish I hadn't done it. I still feel bad. And the day I turned her in… yeah, I cried that day. So much."

"Wow, that's intense."

"You're telling me."

"Sometimes doing the right thing isn't as black and white as people make it out to be."

August wiggled her hips, nudging them against Jack. He wiggled back, and she found his movements oddly reassuring. "A life lesson I had to learn the hard way. Now I'm an even bigger outcast at the firm. But at least I have Christmas, right?"

"You've got friends."

"Yeah, Olivia and Elliot. They took me in during college. Even though I'm an oddball. You may have noticed."

"I think you're beautiful."

She blushed. "You have to say that. You just gave me an orgasm."

"And I'd do it again." His hands roamed up her belly, fingertips sliding just below the under swell of her breasts. "And again and again."

"Call me beautiful or give me an orgasm?"

"Either. Both. All of the above."

He ran his thumb up the ridge of her cheekbone. "You have these freckles here, all along the bridge of your nose. Like being sprinkled with cinnamon."

That feeling that had fluttered in her belly when she'd first met him fluttered again, deeply and curiously.

She looked at him earnestly, unsure how to parse through the feeling. But a yawn hit her hard sending a wave of exhaustion through her warm body. The sun had set over the winter horizon and it was toasty inside the house despite the whirling blizzard around them. She'd never felt safer with a person, her own cozy winter cocoon. A person she barely even knew, no less! More than that, she'd never felt more sated. Her eyes began to droop, the vision of the beautiful man next to her blurring to a hazy dream.

And then, everything went black.

Chapter 6

Q*UITE LITERALLY, EVERYTHING WENT BLACK.*

"Fuck, we lost power." A blanket of total darkness befell Augustn and Jack, the only light peeping in from the last shards of sun through the window.

"Fuck, fuck, fuck." August sat straight up in the bed, holding her towel tight around her. "I need my clothes. We're going to freeze in here. Fuck. Temperatures are in the twenties tonight. Fuck, shit, fuck. What if we die? I can't die of hypothermia, I keep my thermostat at seventy-three!"

Jack got up, helping to collect her sweater from the ground. She shuffled around frantically, her hands skimming the dark and unfamiliar terrain of the floor for her clothes.

"We're not gonna die. There's a fireplace in the living room." Jack tapped her on the shoulder, holding out her pants and sweater. She grabbed them, turning around and stabbing her legs into her jeans and yanking the sweater over her head.

"I don't know how to start a fire! I wouldn't make it as a cavewoman! I'm an accountant!" Her face poked through the collar of her shirt, and she flipped her hair out. "Do you have a match? Do you have fire kindling? Chopped wood?"

He reached out, turning her to him, and placed his hands

on her upper arms, rubbing up and down. "Shhh. Shhh. Shhh. Relax, relax, relax. I can handle it. I know how to use a fireplace."

"What do you have to do? Rub some sticks together?"

"What?" he asked, amusement tinging his words. "No, it's a gas fireplace. As long as the propane tank is filled, we should be good."

"Just in case I think we should put on our winter coats, layer up on pants and sweaters and socks and…Uh no. Will the bedrooms be too cold to sleep in?" She was panicking.

"I have a subzero sleeping bag in my truck for emergencies."

"Bring it in. Just in case." Instantly her mind went to sharing a sleeping bag with him. She didn't even know what kind of sleeping bag it was. Probably a big one. He was a big guy. Would they both fit? *Would he fit…*She shook her head, clearing her mind. *Not like that, August. Not right now.*

She hurried down the stairs, her hand grazing the wall to guide her in the near darkness, Jack behind her. She grabbed her coat and mittens and hat from the coat closet, zipping up over her sweater. She wrapped the scarf tight around her neck and then shoved her hat on. Instantly she felt stuffy and hot as the house hadn't cooled down even a degree yet. But this was anticipatory warmth. She'd get ahead of the problem.

"I'll go get the stuff out of my truck," Jack said, and she heard the sound of the front door close as she was busy tapping away to her group chat.

August: Holy shit! The power's out! What if I die? What if everyone dies?

Elliot: I mean, we're all gonna die.

Olivia: You're not gonna die! It'll come back on.

She looked up to the ceiling, darkness surrounding her. Then she tapped away at her phone again.

August: Also, I have a confession to make.

Both lines of bubbles populated at once.

Olivia: You kissed Jack.

Elliot: You fucked Jack.

An unladylike chortle came from her mouth.

August: So, what do I do now?

Elliot: Bitch, how dare you act nonchalant. I'm gonna need details. It sucks over here. And I lost track of the hot guy. Never even figured out his last name. Next time I get the chance with a hot guy like that I'll be sure to steal his wallet.

Olivia: Classy. And yay! I'm so happy things are working out with you and Jack. I knew you'd like him, Augie! I knew it the moment we met at the bar. He's got great hair too. Super thick, and he takes good care of it. You know what they say about a man who takes care of his hair right?

August: *???*

Elliot: He gives good head.

Olivia: He gives good head.

The screen exploded in fireworks.

August laughed, shaking her head. She loved her friends. And even when they were apart, they were always close.

Olivia: Do you think it's love?

Elliot: Love? Let the woman breathe.

Olivia: Hey, I gotta talk later. Not trying to ghost on y'all, but Henry is driving me up a wall. I have to share a fucking hotel room with him. Can you believe that? August. Your brother is nice but this is awkwaaaaard.

August lifted her brow. For some reason, she didn't quite believe what Olivia was saying about Henry. But she'd leave that for another day because Jack returned from outside with a sleeping bag rolled up beneath his arm and a flashlight peeping out of his pocket. He rubbed his hands together and toed off his boots..

This time she felt completely different about him walking through the door.

"It's crazy out there."

"I know. Everyone is safe though, I just talked to them." She shoved her phone into her pocket.

"Glad to hear it." Jack knelt in front of the fireplace with a lighter and fiddled with some knobs until she heard a clicking noise and a whoosh. The dark room lit up with a warm orange glow at the epicenter. She almost applauded when he stood up and gestured towards the fireplace. He set a flashlight down on the coffee table.

"Holiday's okay?" she asked. It wouldn't do to have a kitten freeze to death inside the house either.

"I'm gonna get her out of her pen and keep her with me."

"Okay. I don't think she likes me very much."

"If it gets cold enough in here, she'll like you plenty."

Jack wrapped Holiday in one of the small fleece blankets in her pen and then sat down on the couch patting the seat next to him.

"I just remembered something," she said as soon as she sat down.

"What's that?"

She turned to look at him, the soft light of the fireplace casting his face in a beautiful glow, catching the auburn streaks of red in his hair. His five o'clock shadow was even darker now. "I have marshmallows."

He smiled. *He smiled a lot.* "Perfect."

She rubbed her hands together. "Does hot chili honey pair well with toasted marshmallows?"

He rubbed his chin, considering her question. "Only one way to find out."

Chapter 7

THE HOUSE HAD SETTLED TO A CRISP CHILL, AND THE COFFEE table was covered with remnants of what looked like the party of an eight year old, minus the quarter empty bottle of gin which they'd gotten into a few hours after the marshmallows.

One furry paw rested gently against August's cheek, as she strained her eyes to find Holiday in a blanket-ball right by her face. Jack was right, Holiday did warm up to August as the temperature dropped.

August wiggled, but she was squeezed tight. She and Jack had slept squished together in the sturdy sleeping bag. His arms were wrapped around her torso, holding her against his hard chest. They weren't naked at the moment but she hadn't forgotten about what it was like to be naked with him.

They'd fallen asleep in their sweaters and sleepy-pants and wool socks. Not sexy, but so very cozy.

When she squirmed, he squeezed her tighter. The tepid morning sun was breaking in light blue streaks through the window, although it was still dark inside the house. The morning chill prevailed over the still crackling fire. She worried about the fire burning all night, but then she decided she'd rather risk fire than freeze to death.

She also really had to pee. How much liquor had they consumed last night? Enough to give her a headache but still not enough to keep her sleeping past her usual wake up time. Damn her very punctual brain. She woke up every morning at six thirty on the dot, no matter what.

She squirmed again and again, but Jack squeezed her tighter, as if a reflex. His hand was on her ass cheek and he gave it a heavy squeeze as well. She warmed a bit at that. She liked the pressure of his body around her. Liked the pressure of the sleeping bag. But she did *not* like the pressure of her full bladder.

"Hey, lemme out…" she muttered.

Jack's eyes fluttered a bit and then the corners of his lips curved genty, as if he was happy to remember where he was.

She tried elbowing her way out but he squeezed tighter again, she was worried she might pee on him. "I have to call the girls…"

"Nooo…" he murmured into her neck sending shivers right down her spine.

"And you…have to…" she finally managed to break her arms free from both Jack and the sleeping bag. "You have to take care of the wild animal you brought in the house."

Jack rubbed his eyes as she shimmied her way out of the sleeping bag. His lips were puffy with sleep, his eyes a little red, his thick dark hair a wild mess. He ran his hands through the tuft at the front cresting it upwards like a wave.

Even with the fire, the morning was frigid, and she wrapped herself in a blanket as she tiptoed her way out of the living room. Then with hastened steps into the master bedroom, she pulled her phone from her waistband.

She went to the bathroom, grateful the water still worked and then quickly tapped out a message to Elliot and Olivia.

August: Any luck over there? Power's still out over here, but we have a fireplace.

Olivia: Oh no! But a little romantic…no? I got no sleep at all. Your brother snores like a buzzsaw.

Elliot: Well, I'm not sure who has it worse. Oh wait, it's def me. Slept in the first class lounge. Feeling grimy af. Still not sure when I'll be getting a ticket out of here.

August: Miss you guys.

Olivia: Miss you, too, Augie.

Elliot: Okay, okay. Forget about us. Did you fuck him yet?

Olivia: Subtle

August: I did not fuck him.

Olivia: Yet…..?

Elliot: Booo!

Olivia: You're doing just fine, sweetie, don't even worry about it. Do what feels right for you.

August: I've just never slept with someone so soon before.

Olivia: Jack's not a stranger! He's a friend.

Elliot: Sleeping with strangers is like one of life's few pleasures.

August chuckled a little at that.

August: Feels very vulnerable. But I like him, you were right.

Olivia: I knew it!

Elliot: Here's what you do: trip and fall on his dick. Bounce up and down a few times. Viola.

Olivia: How is that helpful?!

Elliot: Can't overthink these things. Believe me. Especially not August. She does more thinking than the two of us combined. Although, that's probs not that hard.

A soft knock came at the door. August's tapping fingers froze.

August: Uh oh, gotta go.

Her phone buzzed a few times but she'd already pocketed it into her winter coat.

"Yes?"

The door cracked open, and Jack stood at the threshold wearing navy sweatpants, a grey sweatshirt, thick wool socks and a wool cap. He also wore wool gloves, the kind that had the fingertips cut off. She blushed at the very thought of his fingertips.

"Coffee? I can heat some water over the fire."

She crossed her legs. Uncrossed them. Crossed them again. "How primitive. Yes. Please. I need a few minutes to freshen up."

"Well, lemme see what else I can scrounge up." And then he swiftly crossed the room, leaned over, and kissed her on the forehead. Her jaw practically dropped to the floor. "What was that for?"

He shrugged. "I dunno. I just like you."

"You *like* me?"

"Yeah." He absently brushed away a strand of hair from the side of her face. "You're cute."

Cute? No one, not even her mother, had ever referred to her as cute.

Then he gave her a little smirk and walked right out the door like that wasn't the craziest interaction of her whole entire life.

AFTER AUGUST HAD CLEANED herself as best she could with the freezing cold water, she wrapped herself in the warmest sweatpants and sweater she could find and made her way around the living room to the kitchen.

Jack had plated whole strawberries dipped in granulated white sugar so they looked like they had little snowy tips, with thinly cut slices of kiwi fanned out like flowers, and chopped bananas sprinkled with flax seed on a plate along with a stack of poptarts. She chuckled at the poptarts.

Black coffee steamed from double paned glass mugs next to the food.

"There you are." Jack passed August a plate. "Hope you're hungry."

He followed close behind her to the living room couch, the fire blasting full force. Day had fully broken and they were no longer relying on the light from the fire or their one flashlight. They both sat down on the couch.

With the dawning of a new day, August wasn't sure if they should be touching or not so she left space between them.

But Jack leaned back, stretching his arm around her, casually holding his coffee mug in the other hand. *Oh.* Almost instinctively, she scooted closer, hip to hip with him. He seemed so relaxed in front of her. It was a state she could not claim herself, but she wanted it.

She bit into the corner of a poptart. Blueberry. "I wonder if it'll warm up at all. Winter is so cold," she almost laughed at herself for the silly, awkward small talk she was making.

"I haven't checked…" he murmured, his hand playing with the hair at the nape of her neck. Heat rose to her cheeks and a faint warmth not caused by the fireplace brushed over her skin. Her eyes were going droopy before she could snap out of it.

"Siri, check the temperature," she called out distractedly to her phone which was resting on the coffee table.

"Reading text messages," Siri responded. "Two messages from the group that contains Olivia Couper and Elliot Sheer."

August's eyes shot wide. "What? No, no message, Siri! No message.

But Siri kept speaking in her stilted, robotic tone. "Olivia Couper says: I think it's great you want to fuck Jack, face with heart eyes, face with heart eyes, face with heart eyes. Elliot Sheer says: Just be sure to wear a rubber, thumbs up emoji."

"Siri! Stop reading message! Siri, cancel messages!"

But Siri did not stop. "Would you like to respond to the group that contains Olivia and Elliot?"

"Shit," August dropped her face into her palms, shaking her head. She could feel the movement from Jack, his shoulders shaking. A rumble of a laugh coming from his chest.

Slowly, he pried one hand from her face and then the other, curling a finger under her chin and raising her gaze to his. Then he traced the outside line of her cheek, sliding over the curve all the way to her ear. "So you wanna fuck me?"

She squeezed her eyes shut. "No, don't be silly. I mean yes. Yes, I do. It's obvious, is it not? Siri doesn't lie! And I mean… I did all that other stuff with you."

"Doing that other stuff doesn't necessarily mean you want more."

"No?"

"No." He shook his head then his hand fell and found her knee, patting it softly. "You wanna know why I like cats?"

She thought for a beat. "Yes, actually."

"Cats respect their own bodily autonomy above all else, and that's why a lot of people don't like them. People have this idea that cats are these fickle or solitary creatures. But that couldn't be further from the truth."

"Oh?"

"Cats are clear about what they will or will not consent to. And if you respect their boundaries, you'll have a friend for life. And not one of those shitty fairweather friends. A real, true friend."

"You want to respect my boundaries."

"And I want you to respect mine."

"Have I crossed them?" she asked, alarmed.

He laughed softly, shook his head. "No. But these conversations are good to have. You remind me of a cat. And I like cats. Just like you."

She glanced down at her hands. "That's the nicest thing anyone's ever said to me. A little strange. But nice."

Then he pinched her chin, lifting her gaze so she had to look at him. "And I wouldn't mind if you scratched me up a little too."

Adrenaline shot right through her system.

Fuck it.

She leaned in and kissed him long and slow. She could feel the gentle inhale of his breath and his hands came to either side of her face, threading his fingers through her hair. In that moment she felt unfathomably un-self-conscious. She felt embodied. Grounded. Alive for the sake of living.

"I wanna fuck you."

Chapter 8

How had August gotten here, straddling this strong man, with her thighs wrapped in a vice grip around his hips?

But she couldn't recount the whirlwind hours right now, she was busy.

Hurriedly, she pulled down Jack's sweatpants. He wasn't wearing boxer briefs, actually he wasn't wearing anything underneath. She wasn't wet yet, but she knew it was only a matter of minutes, or seconds. His hands came to the waistband of her flannel pants. They weren't cute but they were comfortable and warm and she hadn't planned on anyone seeing them. He yanked them down as well, his hand finding her hot center His fingers gently rubbed the sensitive folds of her pussy, the sensation falling somewhere between a tickle and pain.

"You're so good at that."

"You're so good at taking it."

Then his dick was sliding against her and her hips were rolling, she grabbed onto his shoulders, her head falling back, breath coming in soft pants. Just like that moisture came rushing between her thighs. "I'm ready, put it in."

"You sure? We just started."

His fingers continued to tease her and she squirmed. She leaned forward catching his lips in a luxurious kind of kiss, the soft lingering kind with a flick of the tongue and a longing for more.

"Guess I'm putting it in."

She lifted up on her thighs to provide space in between them, and he fisted his cock so that its hard length was vertical and ready for her to sink onto. Slowly, she lowered herself, letting the head push through.

Her breath caught at the penetration, and he let out a groan that sounded like painful relief, his fingers digging into the flesh at her hips.

This didn't feel like Ed from the accounting convention. This felt like Jack with the magic cock. And hands. And tongue. This felt new and exciting and different. He'd made her come before, but could he now? Penetrative sex had always been a particularly boring experience for her.

"Take it slow…" she heard his voice through her haze. Once again, she remembered that she was in her own body. And she actually wanted to be there.

Inch by inch she slid down his cock. "God, your pussy is taking me so good," he murmured until he was buried all the way to the hilt and they were flush against each other.

"Good girl. You took the whole thing. You're so good at taking this cock…"

His dirty words both excited and embarrassed her. She almost giggled but choked on it when he began to move, bucking upwards and prompting her to bounce on him like a marionette.

"This okay?" she asked, her head drooped to the side, eyes glazed.

He stroked her hair, moving it off her shoulder and then gripped a fistful of it firmly at the base of her neck just like he'd done in the kitchen. "Don't you worry about me. *Only*…" Thrust. "*Worry*…" Thrust. "*About*…" Thrust. "*This*." He jutted his hips, penetrating her deeply. She let out a cry in response to the spark of pleasure, meeting him at each juncture.

"I've never come during sex before…" she panted.

"Do you have a vibrator?" he asked, which was a silly question to her.

"Of course…but…it's…all the way…over there…" as she bounced she let her hand weakly point towards her bedroom. She'd never used a vibrator with a man before.

He licked her ear, his hand roaming to grab her breast and pinch one of her nipples. The feelings in the base of her stomach began to stir and mix with the feelings near her clit. "I'll have to remember that for next time…"

Next time? He thought there would be a next time? But also did that mean it wouldn't happen this time? The very thought made her heart sink.

"Guess we'll have to do things the old fashioned way." He licked his index and middle finger and reached into the small space in between them. Their skin was slick with sweat now. "Whatever you do, don't stop to think. Any thoughts…just ride them away right on my dick…"

Then his fingertips found her clit, circling in an urgent but also relaxed motion. The combination of being filled to the brim, the motion of his thrusts and the slick stimulation of his fingers was definitely going to send her over the edge.

Wasn't it?

Don't think, just ride.

She was good at taking direction. She was good at giving direction. She tightened her grip on his shoulders.

"Press harder…" she directed him. "With your fingers. And…and kiss me."

An almost dazed smile crossed his face. "Good girl…" he murmured as he leaned in to kiss her, whispering words against her mouth. "You're taking my dick so good…No one's ever taken it so good before…How's that feel?"

He ducked his head lower, his tongue finding the sensitive

tip of her breast. He flicked it in rhythm with his thrusting until her eyes rolled back in her head. She was nearly lost, but she wasn't gone yet.

"How's it feel for you?" she panted, concern rose in her chest. Maybe she was the only one feeling this way?

"Don't ever worry about me…" He gave one particularly good thrust to punctuate the end of his sentence and popped off her nipple.

"I…." she began to stutter, she wasn't sure what she wanted to say because every word had left her brain. "I…" She stuttered again, but inside her body a wave was threatening to rise up within her. She pressed her tongue hard against the roof of her mouth.

And the culmination of every feeling in the world hit her all at once.

"It's gonna happen," she let out a gasp, her body tensing uncontrollably.

His hand reached around her waist, fingertips digging into her soft flesh, pressing her so hard against him, she felt like they might now be permanently suctioned together.

"Good girl, good girl….you're doing so good…I know you're going to come so hard for me…" he murmured the words of praise like she was actually doing something that pleased him.

And she realized…she was….she didn't stop. She kept her hips rolling, letting his fingers slide around her, until that stirring in her belly was bigger than a blip and now becoming a wave. The sensation shot up the center of her body, emanating from her clit and making its way all the way to the roof of her mouth.

She let out a guttural sound, wretching forward against him.

"That's it baby…." he soothed. "Keep on riding…you can do it…keep on riding…Ride it out…"

"Oh, *fuck*." Another wave hit her hard, taking her breath

away. The full feeling of his cock and the rocking sensation of his hips and the circular stimulation of his fingers were wringing more out of her than she even knew was possible.

Then finally, with one more stroke, she was spent. She collapsed against his shoulder, her body a limp noodle. He slowed his thrusts.

"You good?"

She lifted her head. "Huh? Yeah, yeah....I'm great." She rolled her hips lazily on him. "Now you. You come."

"Yes, ma'am." And she watched him, her hand balancing her weight against the top of the couch, holding on for dear life as he thrust into her several times before his thrusts grew erratic and deep, and finally he let out a guttural sound so deep that it was almost like a growl. He squeezed her so tightly to him she thought she might pass out. Until finally, he too let out a long exhale, his muscles going slack.

The juncture between them was wet and hot and slick. She knew his come was leaking out of her. And she didn't care. In fact, she liked it.

An indeterminate stretch of time passed with their bodies locked together. When another reality about bodies began to sink in.

"I have to get up," she whispered.

He squeezed her. "Stay...stay,stay..."

"I'll get a UTI."

He chuckled. "Thirty more seconds."

And then once again, he kissed her on the forehead.

Chapter 9

A FEW HOURS LATER, A DRESSED AND SATED AUGUST FELT LIKE she was in a dream. A very cold electricity-less dream, but a dream nonetheless. More half eaten packaged snacks were splayed across the coffee table, shiny wrappers decorating the surface like Christmas tinsel. Jack confessed that while he might be a fancy chef at a fancy restaurant, when left to his own devices he mainly consumed junk food.

He was even laid back about food. August appreciated that, it allowed her to relax, not think so hard about how she was coming across to him. And there they lounged, August, Jack, and Holiday on the couch under the pile of blankets they'd collected throughout the bedrooms.

Olivia and Elliot texted intermittently. Even Henry texted. As a rule, August and Henry only ever texted each other to complain about their mother. Otherwise, they kept out of each other's hair.

And there was good news. The snowfall had significantly decreased. The plows were doing their jobs. The roads would open soon.

In a funny way, August kind of wished that it wouldn't. She liked being bundled up in front of the fire with Jack. She even liked the small little kitten who cuddled up with them. Jack had been right, Holiday was growing on her, and she thought vice versa. Holiday had to be one of the most affable cats she'd ever met. Not that she'd known that many cats in her life. She was starting to think she'd misjudged them as standoffish and cranky - kind of like her.

Eventually, with too much food in her belly, August felt her eyes drooping and her head getting too heavy to hold up. Jack sidled closer to her and stretched his arm out to wrap around her shoulders. "Put in some hard work this morning..." he murmured.

She was too tired and self-satisfied to blush. The brisk air surrounding them contrasted with the warm coziness of their two bodies huddled beneath the blankets.

A temporary salve to all the wrongs in August's world.

Her stomach turned a little when memories of her reality at work traveled back to her brain. But Jack nestled his nose into the hair at the side of her neck, and before she knew it, those bad memories floated away like so many snowflakes in the wind. For now, at least. And before she could stop it, she was dozing to the gentle heat of his breath on neck.

JUST A FEW MINUTES LATER, August awoke to the high pitched beeps of every appliance in the entire house. The white noise whir of the heater contrasted sharply to the silence right before it. And the lights blared loud and bright.

"Whawuzthat?" Jack's sleepy face popped up from the headrest of the couch, but August was bright eyed.

She wrestled out of their blanket pile and raised her arms as if worshiping the gods of electricity. "It's back. It came back."

Jack was slower to rouse but he got up too and caught her by the waist. "Hot water's back."

"Yes. It is."

He got a deviant glint in his eyes. "Shower?"

"I don't think I can handle anymore sex."

"Who said anything about sex? Maybe I like being extra clean."

Her phone vibrated on the coffee table. She tapped his lips with her finger. "Please hold that thought." And she hustled to get her phone.

Elliot: Bitch I got a flight! I'll be there tonight in t-minus-four-hours.

Olivia: Roads are plowed! Everything's open. See you soon!

Olivia was two hours away. If she and Henry drove extra slow maybe it would take three. All in all, her solo time with Jack was coming to an end. Which was good in a way because she wanted to see all her friends so badly. She even wanted to see Henry.

But also, everyone arriving would definitely put an end to their...*interactions.* Jack lived far away, near Olivia and Henry. And while she might visit every once in a while, she wasn't cut out for long distance. So, that was that for her little holiday fling.

It was probably for the best.

But still...she kicked a fleece blanket to the floor. "On second thought..." She held her hand out and led Jack to the shower.

AUGUST WAS TOWELING off her wet hair and rubbing on some lotion to her damp skin when she heard the door burst open downstairs.

She turned to Jack, in nothing but his boxer briefs, rested against the headboard, lazily watching her as she dressed. He had pushed her against the cold tile of the shower, the hot water hitting her front, then he dropped to his knees and made her come again. She could blush just thinking about it.

And she would think about it. Later, when she was home. And Jack was far, far away. But for now…

"They're here! They're here!" She bounced up and down, clapping her hands like a child, giddy with excitement and the reminder of why she'd planned this holiday to begin with. "Oh god! Put your pants on! They can't see us like this!"

Instead, Jack jumped on her, pulling her into a bear hug on the mattress, the bed already a mess from where they'd fooled around right after their hot, steamy shower together. She let out a loud giggle, the likes of which she'd never heard come out of her mouth before.

"August, hello!" Olivia's cheerful voice sounded down the stairs.

"Get off, get off!" she hissed into Jack's ears, biting back her giggles.

"You already did, baby. Again and again and again…"

She laughed but this time was able to wiggle her way out. Pulling leggings over her still damp body was an obstacle in itself, but she skipped around the room until the stretchy waistband had made it to her waist. She snatched a sweatshirt off the floor and shoved it over her head before she realized it was Jack's.

"Wear it," he said. "Looks good on you."

It smelled like him, spiced ginger and pine, and the inside was so soft and warm.

Then she allowed herself exactly three seconds to admire Jack sprawled out at the end of her bed in his underwear. Now that the heat was running again, there was no need to bundle up like before. In fact, she felt a little overly warm herself. But still, she was keeping that sweatshirt. A Christmas present to remember him by. Surely, she deserved that much.

She bounded down the stairs and rounded to the living room.

Her heart soared at the sight of Olivia and Henry in the entryway.

"Oh my god!" Olivia ran to her the same time she ran to Olivia and they collided in the middle grabbing each other in an aggressive, almost painful hug, jumping up and down in a weird entangled dance.

"Look, I brought us all matching sweatshirts!" Olivia pulled a large weekender bag off her shoulder and yanked out three different sweatshirts with ironed on felt lettering.

The Prettiest Christmas Cunt was Olivia's in a bright pink to match the hot pink streaks she had at the front of her otherwise platinum blond grown out bob.

The Brightest Christmas Cunt was in yellow. That one was for August. Since she was the *smart* one. August used to hate the word cunt when she was growing up. Her mother taught her that she should never swear or speak in a vulgar way. But Elliot and Olivia had partied the puritanical impulses right out of her. And here she was, happily accepting a *See You Next Tuesday Christmas* sweatshirt.

The third read: *The Holiest Christmas Cunt.* August snorted at that one. The bright red color went best with Elliot's jet black hair and bright blue eyes. Yep, that one was definitely Elliot's.

"You really outdid yourself this year," August said to Olivia, and she pulled her in for another hug. Afterwards, Olivia began surveying the scene of the living room. August and Jack hadn't exactly cleaned up yet.

"Wow, looks like you two have been having a whole party without us. Oh my god, Jack! You're here!" Jack appeared at the bottom of the staircase, and Olivia ran to hug him in one of her big bear hugs.

"Wow, Uncle Joe really went all out for you. Must be nice being the favorite even though I'm a surgeon but whatever…" That voice was Henry's. He came in through the front, setting more bags at the entryway and wandered through the living room. His brows were furrowed, analytical eyes examining every decorated nook and cranny. He picked up the corner of a metallic wrapper with disdain. "August, are you eating poptarts?"

Olivia snatched it out of his hand, and gave Henry a pat on the shoulder. "Relax, Henry."

Whatever was going on with Henry and Olivia was *crackling*. She wouldn't ask any questions…Olivia could tell her when she was ready. When or if things were serious. But also, considering this was her brother, she didn't want to particularly know either. She'd leave it at that.

A few minutes later, they were settling in, Christmas carols playing over the speakers, and a simmer pot on the stove. Henry sat on a chair with one ankle crossed over his knee frowning at his tablet, and Olivia was rushing around the living room cleaning up the mess Jack and August had left. Olivia loved aesthetics, and she hated a mess.

"I'll clean up, have a seat…" But Olivia tutted when Jack tried to intervene.

"Don't bother," August said, stroking little Holiday against her chest. "She won't let you. She lives to clean."

"I've tried, believe me I've tried," Henry murmured.

"When have you tried?" Both August and Olivia said at the same time, but then August clamped her mouth shut at the embarrassed look on Olivia's face.

Jack tried to save them with distraction. "Anyone hungry? I could whip up something festive?" But he was ignored.

Henry put down his tablet to meander around the room bending his long frame over the small pen where Holiday was snoozing. "I can't believe there's actually a kitten here. Surprised August didn't make you leave it out to freeze in the blizzard."

"I would never do that to a kitten!" August whacked Henry on the arm. Although, she kind of had suggested just that at first. But in just a few days, she'd changed her mind about the adorable kitten. "Just because I've never had a pet doesn't mean I wouldn't like having one."

"There's the surprise of the year."

Olivia walked by with her dustbuster and threatened Henry with it.

"Hey!" he whined, putting his hands up in the air.

"Don't talk about my friend like that…I'll have to punish you." Olivia glared, making the hand vacuum whir angrily at him again.

They both exchanged what August could've sworn was a spicy expression, but luckily they were all saved by the bell. And that bell was Elliot Sheer.

There was no denying the palpable energy of Elliot when she entered a room, and this time was no different. The front door burst open and metallic confetti flew everywhere.

"Merry Christmas, motherfuckers!" Elliot appeared, in a black jumpsuit, flared pants and a deep Vee at the neckline beneath a large black body length puffer jacket. Behind her Olivia shuffled over with the handheld vacuum and cleaned up the shiny confetti.

"Hey! I was gonna save that," Elliot pouted.

"No you weren't."

August ran over and all three embraced in a big hug, Olivia's hand vac pressed behind their backs.

"The girls are back in town," Elliot said when they relinquished their grasps on each other. Then she gestured towards Henry and Jack. "Plus a few. That's fine. I like the company."

Elliot wielded around and sat on the arm of Henry's chair. "Henry. Good to see you. Looking miserable as ever."

"And you, Elliot. Unhinged as always."

Elliot smiled and squeezed his shoulder.

Then she spotted Jack and gave him a suspicious look. "You."

"Me?" He pointed to his own chest with his thumbs.

"You like my friend?" Elliot asked, gesturing towards August.

"Elliot, please." August protested, although it was in vain.

She didn't want Elliot putting Jack in a weird position. They had already been in enough weird positions the last thirty-six hours.

But Jack handled it, completely unphased. "I do like your friend."

"You wanna date her or something?"

Jack glanced over to August, she knew she must've looked beet red in the face. Then he looked back at Elliot and nodded. "Yeah."

Elliot continued the glare.

"Elliot," August warned.

Then Elliot's face broke into a smile. "You got good taste, my man." And she held her hand up for a high five which Jack met with the correct amount of enthusiasm.

August covered her face with her hands, but Olivia grabbed it away, clasping with hers. "Well, what are we waiting for?" She swung August's hand. "Let's drink!"

Chapter 10

HOLIDAY CHASED AFTER A LONG STRING THAT WAS COMING undone from Elliot's *Holiest Christmas Cunt* sweatshirt. The night was winding down, but Holiday was just winding up now that she'd regained some strength. Although she was still spending most of her time sleeping.

"I wish I could take her," Elliot mused, as the kitten jumped in the air when Elliot dangled the string from her sleeve. "But I travel way too much."

"If you keep letting her play with that sweater she's going to unravel the whole thing," August said, sitting cross-legged on the floor across from them.

Elliot smiled. "Good. I prefer to look like a mess. Wait, I have something better." Elliot plucked a few small Christmas ornaments from a tiny tree on an end table. "Look!" She rolled them across the rug. "She loves chasing after these Christmas balls! Kind of like you, Augie. You like to play Holiday's games too."

"Shut it, Elliot," August said between gritted teeth.

But August warmed at the sight of her friends all in the same place. Henry was hunched over the coffee table, a deck of cards in between him and Olivia, Elliot was playing with

Holiday, and Jack was just arriving from the kitchen with a platter full of snacks he'd whipped up like it was nothing.

She had to admit that she *really* liked him. Just a few days ago, she didn't even know him! But now, they were closer than she was used to. She smiled and happily accepted a small white ramekin filled with a delicate looking crème brûlée topped with raspberries.

Jack had admitted to Elliot that he liked August. But he lived at least three hours away. If nothing else, it was a nice fantasy.

The rest of the evening passed easily. Olivia turned on the Christmas music, dancing in front of the fireplace which made Henry groan, until she grabbed him by the hand and he begrudgingly got up and danced with her in his stiff, awkward way. The women were all wearing their *Holiday Cunt* shirts now. They sang to the familiar songs and took sparkling shots of liquor until they were ready to collapse.

Elliot was wrapped in a blanket next to Holiday's pen, and Olivia and Henry were sitting on either side of the coffee table in arm chairs. Jack and August were on their usual spot on the couch. Jack's hip was almost close enough to press against August's, but still far enough away that they weren't touching.

With surprising disappointment, August realized that she was going to have to go to bed alone. The dynamic had shifted again. She and Jack weren't exclusively flirting and hooking up. There was a whole group of people to account for now. She wasn't entirely sure how to navigate it.

It was one thing that her friends knew she hooked up with Jack, but Henry didn't need anymore details. Plus, was it wrong of her to assume Jack would come to her bed that night? Like he said, just because a person agreed to one thing, didn't mean they agreed to another. They'd messed around a lot already. What was even left to do? She hadn't even stepped foot in his room. No man had ever really wanted to spend time with her like that. Probably better if she didn't make assumptions.

"Think I'm gonna turn in." Olivia yawned and stretched her arms above her head. She stood and leaned over and kissed August on the cheek. "Thanks for planning this. I missed you guys."

Then she headed up the stairs.

Five seconds later, Henry stood as well. "Me too," he said, shoving his hands into his jeans and rocking a bit, as if he were trying to be casual. "It's been a long few days."

Then as if on cue, Elliot stood, cupping Holiday to her chest. "I'd be lying if I said I was going to bed. But I feel weird now, so I'm gonna go upstairs with this kitten and stare at my phone until I pass out. G'night!"

August laughed, nervously. But soon enough it was just her and Jack left there together. Again. Nervousness overtook her. "Well…I guess I'd better be off to bed then." She stood and straightened out her sweatshirt.

She nibbled on her lip and glanced over to Jack.

"I'll see you in the morning then?" he asked.

She waited a beat. He wasn't pressuring her, but it was clear she had to give the invite. For whatever reason, even in the reserves of her courage, she just couldn't do it. *Ah!* She was so weird. Such a coward. She turned towards the stairs. "Goodnight, Jack."

AUGUST LAY IN HER BED, wide awake. Her head lolled to the side, illuminating her phone screen to check the time: two thirty in the morning but her eyes felt wired open. All she could think about was Jack. Why hadn't she just put on her brave pants and invited him to sleep with her? God, she was regretting that now. Why was she such a coward?

She needed bravery. She picked up her phone and texted Elliot.

August: Jack is in his room, I didn't invite him to mine.

Elliot: Is it because you love being alone?

August: No, not this time. This was pure cowardice. What do I do?

Elliot: You…go to his room? Knock on the door. That's usually the order of operations for getting laid.

August: I can't do that, it's too late. I let the moment pass.

Elliot: August, I mean this with love. But get the fuck over yourself.

A snort came from her throat. Then she clicked off her screen, flung her legs over the side of the mattress. and slipped her feet into her wool socks. She was sleeping in Jack's oversized sweatshirt and nothing else. His sweatshirt would give her the courage she needed.

She snuck out the door, letting it latch oh-so-carefully so as to not make a noise and then she turned around and—

Bam! Smack dab against a tall body in the darkened hallway. It took a second for her eyes to adjust and recognize the tall lean frame, but then she almost laughed.

"*Henry?* What are you doing?"

"Just going to the…kitchen?"

Right. August stepped around him. "Sure, me too…"

Then they crossed paths, both shuffling away, neither of them heading in the direction of the kitchen.

August reached the end of the hall and gathered her courage. Elliot was right, she was letting her awkwardness overwhelm her actual, very real and visceral desires. She knocked quietly on Jack's door.

When nothing happened, she almost turned around and hurried back to her room.

Grow up, August.

She knocked again just a bit louder. She waited another minute. *Well, it was fun while it lasted.*

Just as she was pivoting on her wool snowflake socks, the door cracked open. She froze, pivoting slowly back around.

And there he was, shirtless in nothing but a pair of navy sweatpants hung low around his hips, his eyes heavy and his hair a mess.

"Thought I was dreaming," he said, rubbing his eyes.

"Can I come in?"

He opened the door and stepped to the side. The inside of his room felt cozy and warm. It smelled like him too, ginger and pine. She stepped over the threshold, and he very quietly closed the door behind her.

He plopped back down on the bed, his back against the wooden headboard and his legs stretched out in front of him, hands clasped. "Well?"

She stood next to the bed. "Well, what?"

He gave a wicked smile and then gestured to his lap. "Come sit on my lap, baby."

She let out a laugh. But then, she bit her lip and almost ran, now that they'd had all these intimate moments together she was almost feeling too overwhelmed to face another. But no, she wanted this.

And so she climbed onto his lap and when he kissed her, she kissed him back. Without hesitation she wrapped her legs around his waist and the rolling began. His erection rubbed against her clit and she was so instantly wet, already having been primed from their activities through the previous days.

Who could stand being this horny all the time?

Without saying a word he lifted up the hem of her sweatshirt, and yanked her underwear aside, gliding his fingertips along the wet, vulnerable skin of her pussy. She heard his deep groan at the touch, and he pulled down the waistband of his sweatpants, revealing the hard length of his cock. Without another word, she lifted her hips and then lowered onto his shaft.

She took him all in one slide. "You feel so good..." she said, breathless against his ear.

"Shhhhh…." he quieted her. "Don't want the others to hear." But she knew he was teasing.

Then, she rode his cock with abandon, holding onto his shoulders, using the lessons she'd learned from before. He groped at her mercilessly, grabbing a handful of her breast, then rotated between grabbing hip and thigh, as if he couldn't get his hands on her enough.

When his hand traveled to the straight line of her pubic hair, her pussy clenched in anticipation. She'd never slept with a chef before but this one really was remarkably good with his hands.

Coupled with him gently rocking into her and the rubbing of her clit, her orgasm began to build. Now that she'd mastered the duet orgasm, she was ready for business and feeling much more confident.

"Mmhmm, mmmhmm…" she mewled. She could tell he was trying to hold back, that he was keeping to exactly the same speed and intensity as before. And because of that, seconds later she was coming. An orgasm rolled through her body so fiercely she found herself gripping at his shoulders, knuckles tense. At the same time, he let out a gasp, burying his mouth into her shoulder, gasping for air, and letting the orgasm rip through him as well.

She collapsed against his chest, and he held onto her tightly. His cock slipped out of her, and although she knew she needed to get up and pee, she was now so tired she could barely imagine standing and leaving the heat of his bed. So she rolled over to her side, and he curled up behind her, and they fit like two spoons next to each other. And before she could entertain another thought, she softly drifted off to a Winter Wonderland of dreams.

Chapter 11

AUGUST WOKE UP IN A CHILL. SHE REACHED HER HAND OVER and patted the empty mattress beside her. Then awareness spread in her mind. She'd spent another night with Jack. And this time it felt different. Feelings rushed over her. She still felt compelled to sneak out without her friends seeing…which was funny, but old feelings of shame died hard.

Then her brain registered that the water was running in the shower attached to his bedroom. She considered joining him again when there was a knock at the door. She pulled the blanket all the way up to her chin.

"Come in," she croaked.

Elliot opened the door, Holiday resting on her shoulder. "I think this cat wants you."

"Really? How'd you know I'd be in here?"

Elliot gave her a look like, *really?* "She's been meowing ever since she woke up. I already fed her, so I think she's just looking for you. You're a mom now, Augie!"

"She's not my kitten. She belongs to Jack." Although, she'd grown pretty damn attached to the little thing in a short period of time. Kind of how she felt about Jack too, unfortunately.

The sound of the water stopped. And seconds later, the door opened. Jack stood shirtless and wet with a towel slung low around his hips. He rubbed another, smaller towel on his neck.

"I didn't know we had company." *We*. As if August wasn't company, she was the same as him.

Elliot lifted an eyebrow. "Just returning your cat. I'll leave you to it."

He gave a look to August, who let out a weird laugh at the awkwardness of the whole situation. Not that Elliot felt awkward in the slightest. Instead,she just sashayed away in her mini silk shorts and *Holiest Christmas Cunt* sweatshirt.

"Guess that's our cue to get up," August said, bunching the big down comforter around her legs.

"Or we could chat for a bit." Jack sat down at the side of the bed where Holiday pounced on the corner of his towel.

Oh no. Here it comes. The talk. He was going to tell her not to be too serious. *Don't get attached. This is just a fling. He lives far away...*

"Chat about what?" she asked.

"I think you should keep Holiday."

Wait, what? "Wait. What?"

He leaned over and stroked the kitten, her back arching and her tail shooting up straight into the air. Holiday rubbed against his hand. "She really likes you, and I get this feeling that maybe it'd be good for you to have her around."

"Are you saying you think I'm lonely?"

"Nah, I'm saying I think you're responsible. And that you'd take good care of her. And that you'd make her happy and vice versa."

She blushed. Loud, vibrating purrs whirred from Holiday who was now approaching August, head butting August's hand with her little face. She'd never considered having a pet before, but she'd grown so attached in just a few short days. Who knew love could work that way? She considered the idea.

Maybe taking care of something and having a little extra company was exactly what she needed to heal her recent workplace traumas. She nodded. "Yes."

"Yeah?"

"Yes, I do want her. It makes logical sense. I work from home two days a week. And...I don't know...I could figure out how to take care of a kitten. Youtube tutorials and whatnot?"

"I mean, I could always help."

She sighed. "From four hours away? That's a nice offer, but it doesn't sound very practical."

"Four hours away?"

"Yes, that's how long it takes to get to Charleston."

"What? I live in Asheville. That's why Olivia invited me. I just moved here, don't really know anyone."

Literally in her town. How had Olivia so poorly articulated this information? But then she remembered that Olivia relayed facts incorrectly all the time.

"You know that I also live in Asheville, too, right?" August over enunciated to avoid any misunderstanding.

Jack's lips curled in a lazy half smile. "Yeah, I know that."

"So, you meant what you said about wanting to date me? When Elliot asked."

He smiled, scratching the top of his head. "Why wouldn't I have meant that?"

"To be crystal clear, when we leave here, you and I are going back to the same town."

He laughed softly. "Correct."

"And we'll see each other again."

"If you want to, of course."

"Are you kidding me?"

"I'm more confused than anything. You didn't know that we lived in the same town?"

"I had no idea."

"I moved here last year."

"How could I have not known that one simple detail?"

"Well, Merry Christmas to us, I guess." He then leaned forward and kissed her. "We can keep playing these holiday games for as long as we want."

She kissed him back, before pulling away and picking up Holiday, holding the fluffy kitten close to her heart. "The best Christmas I've ever had."

About the Author

Cat Wynn lives in a cozy house in Charleston, SC with her long-time partner and two geriatric rescue dogs. She writes late at night on an old couch that should've probably been thrown out five years ago. She's a shockingly good time at parties provided the snacks are good. You can test this theory by inviting her to your wedding.

You can find Cat on most platforms @catwynnauthor. You can also listen to her wax philosophical about romance novels and writing on her podcast Tall, Dark & Fictional. And if you want to know even more about her you can visit her website, www.catwynnauthor.com and subscribe to her newsletter https://catwynnauthor.substack.com/

Acknowledgments

Thank you to all the great people in my writing community who've helped me get this far: SJ Tilly, G.Marie, S.L. Astor, Elaine Reed, Love Mikayla Eve, and many, many more.

And thank you to my cover designer Beatrix Sawad who went the extra mile making sure I actually had a cover for this book.

Special shout out as always to my partner for constantly going out of his way to support me.

And lastly, thanks to my dogs who always keep me company even in the darkest of nights.

Happy Holidays.

Books By This Author

Partner Track

Perdie Stone needs just three things in life: Her forever best friend, Lucille. Their adorable rescue pug, Bananas. And last but not least, a coveted partnership at her Charleston law firm.

A partnership she more than deserves when she goes head-to-head with hotshot Ivy League attorney Carter Leplan on a big case and comes out on top. She didn't think anything would feel better than beating the annoyingly gorgeous lawyer at his own game, but that's before a freak storm leaves them both stranded.

Together.

In the last hotel room.

With only one bed.

It's a one-night stand Perdie isn't soon to forget…especially after Carter turns up at her firm and slides right into the job that should have been hers. And right back into her life—a life she thought she had all figured out.

Holiday Games

After the worst year ever, August Pointe can't wait to spend Friendsmas with her besties at her uncle's mountain house. She could really use the comfort of a few familiar faces. But when a blizzard hits, August ends up stuck at the house with a mutual acquaintance she's never met instead.

But Jack Harris is a hot, TikTok famous chef. And something about his easy going nature and excellent drink making skills are thawing out August's icy exterior. Plus, he's brought a kitten with him!

August is reluctant to get involved, but some Christmas presents are too tempting to keep wrapped up. And her friends think she deserves a little holiday cheer. Still, August isn't sure if it's worth playing bedroom games with a stranger or if she'll just end up doubly heart broken by New Years.

Hotel Games

Hair stylist Olivia Couper can't wait to celebrate Friendsmas with her besties in a secluded mountain house. So, when Olivia asks Henry, her best friend's grumpy surgeon brother, to carpool, she swears it's a matter of convenience and not a bid for Henry's attention.

Sure, they've been hooking up for years, but they always followed one unspoken rule: Never talk about the hook ups.

Unfortunately, a blizzard hits while Olivia and Henry are on the road, stranding them in the last hotel room available. And suddenly, Henry wants to break all the rules.

Olivia's left with a choice: confront her real feelings for Henry or flee to the mountain house with all her walls intact. It's a game she isn't sure she's ready to play and a hotel stay she isn't soon to forget.